**Two uniformed men rushed toward Jamie.**

"Hey, that woman's wanted!" the store clerk hollered.

Jamie turned back to the building. "How does she know who I am?"

"She must've seen your picture somewhere." Out of the corner of his eye, Zack caught sight of the men approaching the door out of the mail center.

"My picture? What about yours?"

"You're the fugitive."

Right. Her case. His job. Somewhere along the lines he'd shifted further into caring for the victim. Woman. Criminal.

"Stop right there!" One mall cop stayed with the clerk and spoke into his radio.

The other closed the distance between them at an alarming rate. "We said wait." The guy grabbed Jamie's injured arm.

"Ow!" She doubled over.

Zack's gut clenched with her cry. "Let her go." He slammed a jab into the other man's jaw, then another punch to his stomach. While the man stumbled back a few steps, the other guard charged through the doorway.

Zack grabbed Jamie's hand. "Come on!"

**Christa Sinclair** moved from New England to escape the harsh winters and settled in Texas once she received her master's degree in education. When she's not teaching high school English or traveling around the world, she's creating brave new characters who overcome danger to find love and to make sure the good guys win. Find out more about Christa at www.christasinclair.com or follow her on Twitter at @writercsinclair.

## Books by Christa Sinclair

### Love Inspired Suspense

*Fugitive Pursuit*

# FUGITIVE PURSUIT

## CHRISTA SINCLAIR

HARLEQUIN® LOVE INSPIRED® SUSPENSE

Recycling programs for this product may not exist in your area.

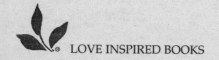

LOVE INSPIRED BOOKS

ISBN-13: 978-1-335-49039-1

Fugitive Pursuit

Copyright © 2018 by Christine Keach

www.Harlequin.com

Printed in U.S.A.

In God have I put my trust:
I will not be afraid what man can do unto me.
*–Psalms* 56:11

Laura Iding and Shana Asaro,
thank you for not giving up on me.

# ONE

Zack Owen had faced some pretty difficult people in his work as a bounty hunter, but no one was more challenging than his older sister when she got an idea lodged in her brain. He tapped his fingers on the steering wheel and rolled his eyes as Lily rattled on.

"I mean, how am I supposed to learn what it's like in the field if none of you will teach me how to be a bounty hunter?"

He stared at her. "You're here with me, aren't you?" Although, now he questioned his decision to bring her along on this fugitive hunt.

After a few moments, she crossed her arms. "Yes, but that's only because you need backup and no one else could come."

His older brothers would kill him if anything happened to Lily. When they opened Second Chance Bail Bonds, they'd all agreed to keep her in the front office and away from the danger. And here he'd put her right in the middle of it.

Bringing Lily along…what had he been thinking?

"Do I get a gun?" Her eyes widened as a huge grin took over her face. It was kind of creepy.

"No. We don't need them. The woman isn't dangerous." He glanced down at the mug shot he'd printed off

the computer before they left the office. After his brothers
reminded him to stay put and out of trouble.

Jamie Carter, arrested on assault charges for going
after a sheriff, now wanted for skipping bail and kidnapping her niece. She was an attractive woman, with sparkling hazel eyes and long hair the color of chestnuts. Her
pretty face made her look sweet and innocent.

Her looks, though, didn't matter. Long ago, Zack had
learned to keep his personal feelings separate from his
professional career. Too much pain was possible when
the two mixed. He'd learned the hard way. In his early
bounty hunting days, he'd foolishly opened his heart to
a woman. Soon, his romance had affected his focus on
the job and an innocent victim had paid the price. Zack
refused to allow that to happen again.

Besides, Ms. Carter had broken the law and Zack
lived by it.

"Remember to let me do the talking, Lil. I'll call you
over to search her when I've got her in custody."

"Okay, but should we have some kind of weapon or
vest?" Lily's hair fell over her shoulder as she glanced
behind his seat. "She *is* a fugitive."

"The woman spends her time with a six-year-old.
She's not likely to have a weapon, if for no other reason
than to protect the kid."

"You're right." Lily nodded as her fingers curled
around the door handle. "Can we go now?"

"Okay." Before he'd finished the last syllable, Lil was
already hopping out of the truck. "What have I done?"
he whispered.

After Zack locked the vehicle, he joined her on the
sidewalk. He folded the mug shot and stuffed it in his
pocket. Like an excited little kid, Lily asked questions,

but she didn't stop long enough for him to answer. Bringing his sister along really had been a bad decision.

Cars rushed by in front of the strip of shops. The scent of newly broken earth from somewhere close by filled his nostrils. Humidity from Rhode Island's annual three-day heat wave clung to his brow and his lip. The heat of the mid-July day suffocated him. A few young women came out of the internet café, giggling and heading their way. Zack tugged the picture of Jamie out of his pocket. "Excuse me, ladies." He made sure his Fugitive Recovery Agent badge was visible. "Have you seen this woman?"

All three of them nodded while one answered, "Yeah, I saw her in here a while ago. I'm not sure if she's still inside."

A jolt of adrenaline rushed through him. "Thank you." His plan had been to check each business and gather as much information as he could about the woman's possible visits to the small town of Trinity. Now, even if Carter wasn't here, he had confirmation that he hunted in the right direction. As the women continued on their way, Zack turned to Lily.

"All right." He pressed his hand on her shoulder. "Here's the plan. You go around to the back door of the café in case she's in here and tries to escape when I walk through the front door."

Lily nodded. "Got it." She fiddled with her bracelet, the one she'd inherited from Mom. "How do I stop her?"

"Hopefully I can talk her into surrendering before you have to do anything." Then he'd only need Lily to pat the woman down. As a courtesy, he and his brothers always had their female partner search the women for weapons. "Go on."

Lily pointed to his hand. "Can I take the picture? I

meant to print a copy for myself at the office but I was so excited I forgot."

He handed it off and watched his sister jog around the corner of the building. Of course, there was no guarantee Ms. Carter was still in here. But sticking his sister in the back, out of the way, was a good decision.

When he reached the windows of the internet café, he pulled the door open and stepped inside. The whoosh of air cooled his damp skin. He stayed at the front of the room and scanned the place: several rows of computers in front of him, a set of copiers near a checkout counter on his left and a section of the room dedicated to a small coffee shop on his right. Fingers tapped against keys. Conversations buzzed around the room. Zack set his fists on his hips. He didn't need the picture he'd given to Lily to know if the woman was in here. He'd studied the attractive face long enough.

From the point of view of a bounty hunter, not as a man. He no longer *did* relationships. Romance included emotions, which led to weakness and he refused to be vulnerable. Once had been enough.

Now, where was his fugitive?

Jamie Carter read the news article on the computer before her. Official reports claimed her sister had had a drug problem that ultimately led to her death. "Yeah, right." Jamie's brother-in-law, Drew, had killed her. Based on her sister's last phone message, Jamie was sure of it. Proving it, though, was a whole other ball game. Tears blurred her vision.

Why hadn't she gone to the house when her sister called?

She swiped her fingers under her eyes. "I'm sorry,

Erin." Sorry for so many things, but mostly for not being there when her sister needed her the most. Jamie had gone on a vacation with her teacher friends to celebrate the end of the school year and to get away from Erin's excuses for staying in the marriage. She'd had enough of trying to convince Erin to leave her abusive husband. When Erin had called and left a rushed message, Jamie hadn't heard the phone ring and Erin had died. Jamie had gone to the house on her way home from her trip, but it was too late. The investigation was underway, with speculation her sister's drug dealer had killed her.

Except Erin didn't do drugs. Never had, never would have.

When Jamie arrived at his home, Drew stood outside, holding his daughter and pretending to mourn his wife. But when Jamie looked into his eyes, she knew he'd had a hand in Erin's death. Like a wild woman, she pushed, punched and swung an IV pole at her brother-in-law and one of the deputies in front of a yard full of lawmen, paramedics and spectators. Of course, the men pressed charges. While waiting to see a judge, Jamie's head swam with indecision. But nothing mattered except honoring her sister and getting her niece to safety.

Quiet sobs stole her breath as memories huddled in her brain. She didn't think it was possible, but again her heart wrenched in her chest. She'd make it up to Erin, though.

A few days after Jamie made bail, she followed her niece and the girl's new nanny to Charlotte's favorite park. Joy traveled through her, and when the nanny got caught up in flirting with a man sitting next to her with a baby on his lap, Jamie pulled her niece and the girl's bedraggled stuffed elephant into her arms. As Charlotte chatted excitedly about how happy she was to see Jamie, she whisked her away. Now she was ready to focus on somehow proving to anyone who would listen how evil her brother-in-law was.

Rumors throughout the small town of Hampton and through some of her students claimed Drew authorized his deputies to sell drugs there and in nearby communities. If she couldn't get him investigated for her sister's death, then she'd work to get him held accountable for the drugs he and his deputies peddled. Jamie's next step was to interview some people. But who? How?

She closed her eyes and lowered her head. From successful, well-respected high school teacher to wanted woman in a matter of weeks. Could she succeed in bringing Drew down? Alone? To her success, everything Jamie set her mind to she achieved. But being wanted by the law...

The bell on the front door signaled a new customer entering.

And God helping her? That wouldn't happen. He'd abandoned Jamie the day He first allowed Drew to steal Erin from her.

The new person, an imposing figure of a man, stood by the door, scanning the room. Jamie tensed. She was pretty sure he wasn't looking for a seat since several near him remained empty. Although he wore no uniform, some kind of badge dropped around his neck.

Right. Time to go. Thankfully her niece was tucked away safely with a friend, so only Jamie had to run. As quickly as she could, she gathered the printouts covering the details of her case since she'd run and stuffed them into her backpack. When she rose from her chair, she kept her gaze toward the back of the room and prayed the man wasn't looking for her.

A burst of air from the vent above her head stirred the strands of hair hanging loose from her ponytail. She fought every nerve to walk casually toward the back hallway.

"Jamie Carter." A deep voice stirred something within her—fear, ease, maybe a bit of both.

Customers nearby stared at her.

She stopped and slowly turned to face the man about ten yards away from her. Dark hair, dark clothes. A few inches taller than her five foot seven, with well-defined muscle in his limbs, he could prove to be a challenge during her escape. She'd never seen him before. Could he be one of Drew's musclemen? Or a new deputy?

"How'd you find me?" Like a wheel, her brain spun, scanning the surroundings, searching for freedom. Leaving by the front door would be impossible.

He shrugged one shoulder. "I asked around. Took a chance you'd be in the neighborhood." When he stepped closer, she could see hair that barely touched his shoulders and a handsome face with a rounded jaw. "I'm sorry about your sister."

A sense of intimacy rolled between them, his words like a balm over her broken heart.

Jamie shook her head. Crazy. The man was the enemy. "Sure, you really care."

"I do. I can't imagine losing one of my brothers or my sister in such a way."

A hint of sympathy passed through his expression, as though he could truly understand her pain. Since when had her brother-in-law hired anyone with compassion? "You can tell Drew I'll never stop fighting him, not until he answers for the crimes he's committed." Abuse, murder, drug peddler. Could there be more offenses?

Being more used to facing teenage drama and too many parent meetings than life on the run, Jamie didn't have all the investigative skills she needed yet to convict Drew. But her time in the education system had taught her to roll with the punches. Hopefully her success rate inside a classroom put the odds in her favor as she attempted to uncover the truth. Nothing would stop her, not even the handsome man in front of her.

"The only person here with a warrant is you." The man inched closer. He remained calm, confident.

She was not.

Going left or right would wouldn't work. Too many people to maneuver around. Any one of them might grab her for him.

"So, what are you going to do? Bury me in an unmarked grave somewhere or take me back to Drew so he can kill me himself?" Several more customers stopped what they were doing. Many chose not to look directly at her. "I'm not going with you."

"You don't have a choice. You kidnapped your niece."

Other people watched her and the man, as though enjoying a tennis match, as their conversation continued.

"I didn't kidnap her. I'm protecting her." Although Drew spent most of his marriage hitting Erin, he hadn't hurt Charlotte, according to the little girl. Jamie had made sure to ask. Often.

He shook his head. "The courts don't agree."

"The courts are full of obnoxious old men who don't have a clue what a true villain Drew Timmins is." When the man took another step toward her, she backed up. "Please. My niece and I are in danger. Don't you have a heart?" *Make a decision.* Which way should she run?

Metal clinked behind her. The closest computer geeks leaned over to glance around her.

Jamie jerked to one side so she could keep an eye on the man while assessing the latest threat. A woman, shadowed by the darkness of the hallway behind her, approached with handcuffs dangling from her fingers. "Please don't make this harder than it needs to be."

"Lil, I told you to wait," the man grumbled.

Okay, if this woman was working with him, then they were definitely not Drew's employees. Her brother-in-law would never hire a woman.

"I thought you and Ms. Carter could use a hand."

Fear shot through Jamie. Once those metal bracelets clinked around her wrists, her attempts to eventually earn Charlotte a safe life would be over.

Which way should she go?

"Let me handle this," the man said through what sounded like gritted teeth. He moved a little quicker but with the hint of a limp.

The woman continued walking closer to Jamie. A few inches shorter, several pounds lighter and with hesitation in her step. If the lady tried to grab Jamie, could she fight her? Adding another assault charge to her growing list of offenses wasn't ideal, but protecting her niece meant more.

Once Jamie had gathered enough evidence of Drew's illegal activities, maybe the charges against her would be dropped. Although, maybe not because she had actually assaulted her brother-in-law. But somehow she'd convince the courts to award her full custody of Charlotte despite Jamie's crimes. Unless God still wanted a good laugh.

"Ms. Carter." The man's voice broke into her thoughts. "Let us take you in and put an end to your running."

"Never going to happen." She shifted her focus to the woman, now within two feet of her. "I'm sorry." Jamie moved forward, slammed her heel onto the other woman's foot and shoved her shoulders back with as much force as possible. While the woman teetered, Jamie crouched down and swiped the woman's feet out from under her. As the lady's body fell backward, Jamie turned and ran.

"Wait!" Zack's gut clenched as his sister fell like a ten-pound bag of potatoes. The metal door from the back of the room slammed against the outside of the building as the woman ran through it. Adrenaline surged through him. Several people from the last row of computers scrambled from their seats and slid in beside his sister. He barely glanced in Lily's direction, though, as he broke into a run after the fugitive.

Heat hit him as soon as he stepped outside. He glanced to his right and saw only an overloaded trash bin. To his left, a car moved slowly as though the driver searched for a parking space. Jamie had just passed it.

Zack took off after her. His badge slapped against his chest. As he moved, he slammed pressure onto a not-quite-healed leg. Pain jolted through his knee from when he wiped out on his surfboard. "Carter!"

The woman rushed between a set of trees at the end of the parking lot, a long ponytail waving behind her. A loose-fitting dark T-shirt and blue jean shorts would help her disappear into the wall of trees, leaving him in the dust, looking like a fool.

Zack stopped running and bent over. He set both hands on his thighs and prayed for the pain in his leg to diminish. What had he been thinking? Stupid decision to come after a bounty with his inexperienced sister and his less-than-ready body.

Yikes. Lily. He'd bailed on her. When he turned around, a sea of faces greeted him from just outside the internet café. Questions flew at him as he hobbled back to them.

"Who was she?"

"What'd she do?"

"Want us to go after her?"

They crowded him as he crossed the back entrance and into the hallway. "It's all right, guys. We'll get her another time." Business patrons passed by him and shuffled through abandoned chairs. Voices buzzed once again.

Several people crowded Lily as she sat in a chair and rubbed the back of her head. "Lil?"

"I'm okay." Once she stood, she closed the distance between them. "What about you?"

He scanned the room. Several people had returned to their work, with the few remaining stragglers backing away. "Kyle was right. I'm not ready to go back in the field." His older brothers had relegated him to the office of their bounty hunting business for another few days, as though he, a grown man, couldn't decide when his body was healed enough.

Clearly, they had a point.

The jabbing pain along his leg dulled to a throbbing ache. He shifted his weight to his uninjured knee.

"Do you want to sit down for a few minutes to rest your knee?"

He shook his head. "No, I'm good. Let's get out of here."

"Don't worry." Lily wrapped her arm around his back

and leaned her head on his shoulder. "We still have the advantage with Carter."

"How do you figure?" Zack steered her toward the checkout counter.

"You were able to find her once. You'll be able to do it again."

"Maybe."

A man around his age rushed to the counter. His name tag read Randy. "How can I help you?"

"Sorry about the ruckus."

The guy waved them off. "Forget it. No one got hurt, which is the important thing."

"Lil, where's the picture?"

Lily pulled the fugitive's photo from her pocket. Once he took it, Zack unfolded it and placed it on the counter.

"We were searching for this woman, Jamie Carter. She's not a dangerous criminal so you don't have to worry. She probably won't come back, but if she does, can you call the number on the bottom of the page?"

Randy held the paper like it was gold and nodded. "Of course, sir, miss." His gaze shifted to Lil. And stayed there.

Zack glanced at her, smiling away, batting her eyelashes at the guy. "Thanks." He pinched his sister's sleeve and tugged her toward the door. "Let's go, *miss*."

Once they stepped outside, Zack grinned. "He's too young for you." He didn't look at her, but from the corner of his eye he could see Lily glaring at him. They walked in silence back to the truck. The wind shook the tree leaves, which created strange sunshine patterns.

Carter had been prettier than her mug shot, even with the worry creasing her brow. In her picture, her wavy hair dipped past her shoulders. Today, she'd pulled it away from her face, which made her look younger than her twenty-four years and much more vulnerable. His heart almost went out to her.

But it didn't. He was a professional and she was his criminal.

Inside the vehicle, Lily met his gaze. "You know the others are going to have a word or two for us, right?"

"Yup." But it would be Zack they'd be angry with, not Lil. A hundred justifications for taking her along on his hunt for Ms. Carter roamed through his head, but none of them would be good enough for his brothers. He shouldn't have gone, they'd say, should've left Lily at work, he'd acted totally irresponsible, blah, blah, blah.

"You can handle it, though. You know you're one of the best and they're only jealous." She clicked her seat belt into place. "Besides, I'm a big girl. I make my own decisions."

Yeah, he'd push that justification. It hadn't been his decision after all.

For some reason, he took one more glance across the parking lot toward the wall of trees. Of course, Carter was long gone. He had to admit, the woman's story intrigued him. So did the worry plastered across her face. Yes, as bounty hunters, he and his brothers heard sob stories all the time, criminals forming paper-thin explanations in hopes of gaining an ally, but Jamie Carter's impassioned plea had caught him off guard. What if the woman spoke the truth? What if she did everything she could for an innocent kid?

Nah. Just because he hadn't been out on the hunt in almost four weeks, he couldn't let his brain freeze. Besides, the courts called Jamie Carter a criminal who needed to be brought to justice. He had to follow the law.

\* \* \*

Two days later, Jamie sat on the blanket she'd set beside her tent and leaned her head against the tree. Excited voices of adult campers and children around her helped to calm her heart. Yes, she could've hidden farther into the woods, where no one would find her, but the complete human stillness would leave her with too much time to think. Guilt had a way of creeping through silence.

What was she doing? By walking away from her sister and having fun on a vacation, she'd managed to let one of the most important people in her life get hurt. No, both people if she thought about it. Her sister was dead and her niece had no parents. Well, technically Charlotte still had a father, but if Jamie had her way, the man would never see his little girl again. Drew wasn't fit to be a father.

Giving up her comfort in her apartment once she'd gone on the run had been a no-brainer. But she hadn't been prepared for life as a fugitive. She constantly looked over her shoulder, and in another night or two, she'd have to move again to another campground. Too much time in one place made her an easier target to find.

When she and Erin were little, they used to put up tents in the backyard and treat their evening like a grand adventure. These days she was also on a journey but one of a whole different kind.

When she took Charlotte and jumped bail, she knew she had to let go of anything normal—no cell phone, no personal computer, no familiar places. She had grabbed the basics for survival, dropped her niece off with a friend willing to help and pitched her tent in the city park. With a beach on one side and summer campers on the other, she hid out, hoping for the guilt inside her to tamp down in her brain long enough for her to find a way out of the mess she was in.

As a soft breeze floated through the leaves, she glanced around the trees. Sunshine created streaks of light across the dirt paths, reminding her of the joy and happiness bubbling throughout her and Erin's adventures all those years ago. Soft and comfy sleeping bags had cradled her and her dreams.

Now, she was alone.

Once she put Drew behind bars, she and Charlotte would camp throughout New England, hitting all the best-known parks. Jamie would make sure to share her sister's love of camping with the little one.

She scrubbed her palm over her face and shifted her gaze to the wallet-sized picture of her, Erin and Charlotte that she kept in her backpack. Inside the bag were a few changes of clothes, all the money she had in her savings account and everything she held dear: pictures, Erin's favorite Bible, trinkets that friends and family had given Jamie over the years, her own journal documenting her emotions as well as her ideas about Drew's failings as a sheriff…and as a man.

Men were supposed to love their families, take care of them, cherish them.

Drew protected himself and his reputation.

Her thoughts drifted to the bounty hunter who'd tried to capture her the other day. He was probably good to his family. He seemed to care about following the law, not abusing it. What would it be like to have a man like him in her corner? She pressed her back to the thick tree stump as the image of the man flooded her brain. Of course, it didn't hurt that he was easy on the eyes.

But Jamie had no time for romance. Thoughts of Mr.

Bounty Hunter were a luxury she couldn't afford. She needed to stay focused on making up for her mistake, for not being there when Erin needed her most.

Jamie hadn't heard her ringing phone while at breakfast with her friends on the last day of vacation. Before she got on the road to return home, she'd listened to Erin's message.

She was ready to leave the marriage, she'd found some incriminating evidence of Drew selling drugs and she needed Jamie ASAP. Noises in the background made Erin whisper and rush her words. She told Jamie she loved her. She started saying something about Mrs. C., an old family friend, but her words were cut off, then the phone had gone dead.

Charlotte, though, the most important person in Jamie's world, was safe. Jamie wished she could stop by her friend's house to spend some time with the girl, but she'd never put the child in unnecessary danger. Plus, Greta lived in Massachusetts. The time it would take to get there was precious. Jamie needed to stay focused.

With a heavy sigh, she returned the picture to her backpack, then stretched out on her back. Sunshine through the leaves cast heat and brightness over her. Jamie closed her eyes and willed herself to relax.

With so much pain in her heart, such weariness in her muscles and so many unanswered questions, being at ease seemed a million miles away. *Hey, God, do You think You could guide me through this journey so I can protect Charlotte and honor my sister?* She was pretty sure He didn't care about her, but Charlotte? Surely God could come through for a beautiful child.

For a few hours, she'd rest, then she'd head to her grandmother's best friend's house. Another neighbor had said Mrs. C. had been gone for a couple months, but she was due back from visiting her son sometime today. Maybe the woman had evidence against Drew that Erin had started gathering while Jamie was out gallivanting with her friends? Surely Mrs. Cecily could give Jamie some insight into…something…

Maybe.

The weight of her battles pushed against her shoulders. Putting up with teenage attitudes, she could handle. Investigating a killer and possible drug pusher, though, was she good enough?

Yeah, her job. Only three years in the classroom and after all her questionable choices lately, she might never be allowed inside a school again. Thankfully she was on summer break, so she didn't have to consider having a meeting with her boss. At least, not until August. She prayed her boss would show understanding and welcome her back when Jamie put Drew away. *If.*

Jamie flattened her palms on her stomach. A few minutes of nothingness and then she'd start planning her next move. For a few moments, she just needed…to be.

Something interfered with the brightness of the sun. A shiver scaled her spine. She jerked upright and scanned her surroundings.

A blue jay chirped above her.

She tossed the tent opening to one side and grabbed the baseball bat one of her star students had given her when he got accepted to his favorite college with a baseball scholarship. Wrapping her fingers around the base, she slid behind the biggest tree trunk nearby. Could Drew have found her? But she'd been so careful.

Faint hints of movement within her camping space broke down her confidence.

Did she dare peer around the trunk?

With the bat hanging over her shoulder, she inched forward enough to see an empty spot. She moved a little farther.

But the bat stayed still. "Your time on the run is up."

Her heart jumped. She jerked her head around. Before her stood what looked like close to two hundred pounds of muscle. The man from the internet café two days ago. The injured one. The handsome bounty hunter. A hint of relief spread out through her chest. At least it wasn't Drew.

Still, ways to escape his custody surged through her mind as she glanced around him. She'd done it before. She could do it again. Hopefully. Although this time he had her pinned to the trunk of a tree. A hint of cologne or soap drifted to her nose.

"I see the look in your eyes." He tugged the bat out of her hands and tossed it behind him. It landed by her backpack. "But you're not going anywhere except to jail."

Anger for the way she'd left him at the café should have been visible through his expression, but he studied her with calm determination. He was bigger than she'd first thought the other day, wider in the chest. Stronger, probably. Intimidating, definitely.

Yet she didn't fear for her life.

Jamie swallowed the lump in her throat. How would she get out of this? "Who are you?"

After taking a couple of steps back, he propped his hands on the waistband of his cargo pants. "My name's Zack Owen. I'm a bounty hunter."

One man trying to finish her off and one trying to bring her in. Great. As if her life wasn't complicated enough.

"How'd you find me?" She'd thought she'd been doing well staying off the grid.

"I asked questions. People around the internet café, people on the bus routes, others by the beach and in the park…they all gave you up."

"How's the woman from the other day? I didn't mean to hurt her. It's just…there's a lot at stake."

"Like you trying to blame everyone else for your behavior?" He reached into his pocket and pulled out a pair of handcuffs.

She lifted her chin. "Not everyone else. Just the man responsible."

"The courts can sort all that out." Leaning forward, he took a loose hold of her arm. "Let's go."

She couldn't explain it, but something about him made her want to trust him, to reach out to him for assistance. Maybe going with him could work in her favor. She spent enough time guiding teenagers to her side of the bargaining table. She could do the same thing with this guy.

Except Zack Owen was no sixteen-year-old. The bottom line was she didn't know this man. Her heart might be urging her to take a chance, but her brain knew better.

She dug in her heels. He stilled, staring down at her with piercing green eyes the color of an Irish countryside. "Look, I won't put the cuffs on you if you can act like a civil human being."

"You can't—"

"Yes, I can." His grip tightened. "Now what's it going to be?"

She nipped her bottom lip. Several seconds ticked by. *Think of something.*

"Come on." He tugged her toward the camping site parking lot, fifty, sixty yards away.

Jamie froze. Two of Drew's men stalked toward them. She couldn't be caught. Charlotte needed her. At least with the bounty hunter she had a chance.

Zack stilled, looked from her to the men. "You know them?"

"Yes. How did they find me?"

"Probably the same way I did."

She gripped his arm. "I'll go with you, but let's go in the other direction." And she'd pick up her backpack on the way. She couldn't leave her most treasured items behind.

"Why?"

"Later." She tried to drag him toward the tent, but the stubborn man wouldn't move.

Big beefy Charlie, an off-duty deputy, closed in. "There you are."

Jamie had seen the man next to him once or twice with Drew. Ben was his name. He pointed at her. "We've wasted a lot of time looking for you."

"Who are you guys?" Zack braced his stance.

Jamie inched closer to him until their arms touched. She wanted to take hold of his hand, but she kept to herself. "They're deputies from my brother-in-law's office."

As though the bounty hunter wasn't even there, Charlie closed the distance between her and himself. "You know what we're here for, Jamie. The kid. Where is she?"

"I'll never give up my niece." She'd die first.

"Sorry, but Jamie's coming with me." The bounty hunter slid her behind him. A wave of relief rolled through her. She pressed her palms to his back.

"Not too many people say no to Charlie." Ben snickered.

Charlie straightened to his full height, only around

five feet eight inches, but his bulk made up for what he lacked in height. "I don't think you understand. We need information from her and we're authorized to get it however we can."

The bounty hunter didn't even flinch. "No, *you* don't understand. Your boss has no legal right to threaten her. As a sheriff, he should know he needs to let the justice system work."

Tension rose like a thick layer of smoke. She'd wanted to get away from Mr. Bounty Hunter, but for the moment he was her only ally.

The other two men chuckled and traded glances. "Get out of my way." Charlie took a swing at Zack. The thwack when Charlie's fist connected with the bounty hunter's jaw resonated through the woods. Zack tossed an uppercut, which snapped the other man's head back.

Guilt rose inside her. No, she didn't want to go with the bounty hunter, but she didn't want him hurt because of her, either.

While Zack tangled with Charlie, Ben marched toward her. Jamie scanned the floor of the woods as she backed up. She needed a weapon. Leaves…rocks…the bat.

Bingo!

She scrambled to reach the bat Zack had tossed aside. Panic flushed through her. Ben yanked on the back of her shirt. "Get over here."

She grabbed the wooden bat, whirled around and bashed it on his arm. The vibration numbed her fingers, her forearms.

The man howled. He cradled his arm close to his chest, then glared at her with fire in his eyes. "You little…" Ben grabbed her again.

Behind them, one of the men thumped to the ground. *Please not the bounty hunter.* Jamie struggled to turn around. Relief flooded her. Zack moved toward Ben, took hold of the man's injured arm and shoved him to the ground. Another howl.

Charlie reached behind him, tugged something free and…aimed a gun at Zack's back.

She released the bat. "Look out!" Jamie knocked her bounty hunter down.

The gun went off.

Zack used his hands to break his fall. Guns? No, this definitely wasn't good. This bounty was a lot more complicated than he'd ever imagined. He should've handed the woman over, but because he cared about the fear he'd seen in her eyes, he was now between a rock and a hard place. With weapons.

Emotions had no business here. He had to think exclusively like a bounty hunter and not as an affronted citizen.

Amid screams and hollers from other parts of the campsite, he pushed himself back up, grabbed the bat and smacked it down on the big guy's hand as he aimed his weapon for Jamie, who remained on the ground. The gun tumbled across the dirt away from the two lawmen. Both deputies scrambled for the weapon.

Zack yanked the woman's arm and got her to her feet. "Go!" She teetered for a moment, then ran to the tent. What was she doing? "Come on, Carter!" It took her only seconds to grab a small, plaid backpack. Then they slid in between the trees, deeper into the brush.

"Get after them!" one of the men yelled from behind. No shots followed. Each second passing without another threat made Zack more nervous. Could he keep himself and Jamie safe?

She shoved a tree branch out of her face as they rushed toward a cabin standing not fifty feet from them. A shot rang through the air. Instinct had him ducking. *God, please guide us to safety.* He hadn't brought his own weapon because he didn't think he'd need it to capture Jamie.

"We're not hiding in there," he said matter-of-factly when they reached the cabin.

"No. Come this way." She rushed around the building and guided him into a denser part of the forest.

"Where'd they go?" hollered either Charlie or the other man from far behind them.

"Head that way!" demanded the other.

Jamie twisted around for a second. Sirens whirred to life in the distance. Fear skidded through her striking hazel eyes. Her skin took on a pasty white color, as though all her blood had dropped to her feet.

He set his palm on her shoulder. "It's okay. We'll get out."

Doubts plagued his mind. Options warred within him. His head said to focus on getting her to the proper police and completing his duty, but his gut demanded he keep the determined woman on the run for her safety. Which was the right decision?

He could turn her over now, but something wasn't right if a couple of off-duty lawmen were ready to shoot first and ask questions later.

Jamie charged along the path laden with trees as though she'd come through here before. But where was she leading him? And how would they get back to his truck?

She stopped. After a heavy breath and a brief moment with her eyes closed, she continued on their trek. He tugged the backpack. "Wait a minute." He leaned against a tree trunk.

Jamie stared at him with her milky white face and a little less confidence. He had the urge to pull her into his arms and be the rock she clearly needed.

Temporarily, of course. Like he'd do for any friend.

A dark red stain on her shirt caught his eye. Blood dripped off the edge of her sleeve.

*What?*

"You're bleeding?" Zack lifted her shirtsleeve. Dark red blood gathered at a gash along her arm. More blood dribbled along her skin. If he hadn't moved when the man had aimed for him by the tent, he'd be bleeding out. If Jamie hadn't pushed him down… She'd taken a hit… for him. For a moment, he was paralyzed.

"I'll be fine." She tugged herself free. "I've had worse." Her gaze avoided him.

Why didn't he believe her? Sickness rumbled through his gut. "Why didn't you tell me you'd been hit?"

"I'm pretty sure it's just a scratch. Can we discuss this later? I'd like to get away without any more injuries." She glanced behind them, then forward. "There's another playground not far from here. You'll be able to take a bus back to your vehicle."

He didn't miss the fact that she skipped talking about herself. She kept her gaze locked with his, as if daring him to argue.

So often his job was black-and-white, right or wrong. After the incidents at her camping site, things had never looked grayer, which was the absolute last place he wanted to be. Emotions led to indecision, which led to vulnerability. He'd successfully avoided that for five years. What was he supposed to do now?

He reached forward to pull a few strands of hair from the corner of her mouth.

She slapped his hand away. Gone from her eyes was any ounce of fear. Survival guided her movements.

He wanted to apologize and yet…he didn't. Instead, he raised his hands in a surrender motion. "If your brother-in-law is such a bad guy, why haven't you gone to the state police?"

"He's got everyone fooled that he's the perfect sheriff, so no one questions him. By the time we realized what was happening in my sister's marriage, it was too late. Things kept getting worse. Erin was convinced to try to make the marriage work, especially when my niece came along. Until…"

"Until what?"

"Before she died, Erin had left me a message. She started telling me stuff."

"About what?"

Jamie shook her head. "I don't know." She returned to their path.

Oh, she was definitely a bad liar. But getting the truth out of her would have to wait. Escape first.

As they silently followed the path through the wooded grounds, Zack's mind whirled with too many thoughts. None of them made sense. *God, I know this bounty run has fallen apart, but I trust in Your guidance.* If anyone could get Zack out of this mess, He could. Hopefully without Zack having to call in his siblings. Because the latest events would not go over great.

Birds chirped as though nothing was wrong. A soft breeze took the edge off the heated afternoon. The scent of barbeque reminded him that he hadn't eaten since breakfast.

The last copse of trees opened to a large park. An area with slides and jungle gyms sat in the center of a bike and walking trail. Children's laughter drifted toward them along with a puppy's bark.

"Hold up." He bent over with his hands on his thighs. If his sense of direction was right, they were still in Champlain Park, the Ponahochet County side, nowhere near his truck. Thankfully his knee had held up in the escape, although a twinge of an ache from his surfing accident remained.

Beside him, Jamie planted one hand on her waist. The other, the one with the injury, hung motionless. The backpack remained slung over her shoulder. Blood continued to drip from under her shirtsleeve. The stain on her shirt had morphed into a mini-explosive pattern. "We need to look at your arm."

Should he apologize for getting her shot?

"Don't worry about it." A hint of blond peeked through the strands of her hair.

"You're bleeding. You look as white as a glass of milk. I'm waiting for you to pass out on me." He pinched her shirt fabric.

She jerked away. "Don't." The word bolted out of her mouth with as much force as the steel in her gaze.

He froze, his fingers a few inches from her. For several moments, they stood at a standstill, but then her gaze softened. "I'm sorry. I know you're trying to help and I do appreciate it."

For the first time, he truly saw the vulnerability of the woman standing before him. The difficulties of being on the run lay across her body, in her choices, through her movements. The bounty hunter in him wanted nothing more than to turn her in. The man in him wanted to tuck her under his arm and whisper everything would be all right.

*No caring allowed. Keep your mind on business.* "Head for the bench over there and I'll take a peek at your wound."

After a glance in the direction of the seat, she scanned the park. She remained rooted to her spot.

"If you run, Jamie, I will catch you."

She brushed her fingers against her temple. He almost had her cooperation. He could feel it in his gut. But why was it so important to him?

"All right." She nodded and walked by his side to the wooden seat. The backpack came off her shoulder, but she kept a tight grip on it. Once she sat, he crouched down beside her and lifted her sleeve. Closing her eyes, she breathed out slowly. Blood had gathered along a gash about two inches long. "It doesn't look too bad." Seared flesh, but no hole. "The bullet grazed your arm. It's not too deep and it's not bleeding anymore. How does it feel?"

"Like someone's stuck me with a hot poker."

He gingerly touched his knuckle to the skin around her wound. She hissed, jerked upright. "Sorry."

"Do you have any tissues in your backpack or something to wipe your arm?" No way would he leave her side to grab paper towels from the restroom close by. He had no doubt she'd be gone before he returned.

"No." She tugged the backpack closer to her, one arm over it protectively.

"What do you have in there? Gold? A wad of bills? Weapons?"

"Some clothes." Helplessness brought moisture to her eyes. "And things more important to me," she whispered.

He almost set his hand on her knee. Almost. "Like what?"

"Pictures of my family, gifts my sister gave me as we grew up, her and my journals from when we were teenagers, things like that." She sniffled and swiped her fingers beneath her eyes. "So, what's the verdict on my arm?"

"You'll live." He released the fabric and stood. "But from the actions of those two guys at your campsite, you're in a lot more trouble than you realize. Definitely more than I thought." After he pulled his cell phone from his pocket, he slapped it in his palm while he paced in front of her. No, he didn't want to call his brothers. They'd probably tell him how foolish he was being, but he needed a clearheaded response.

Jamie's world had shifted upside down, becoming more dangerous than she'd ever expected. "I'm not strong enough," she whispered. She glanced at the red marks on her sleeve, then gently lifted the cloth away from her injury. The skin burned. Like Zack said, she hadn't been shot, but it looked like the piece of metal had singed right past her on its way to a tree trunk. Her brain still shook with the reality of being so close to dying, to breaking her promise to her sister.

The urge to hug her niece, to hold her close, took life within her. Did Charlotte wonder where Jamie was? It had been two and a half weeks since she'd left the child in another state with someone Charlotte had never met. Did she wish her aunt instead of Jamie's best friend from elementary school was the one reading her stories as she drifted off to sleep?

Jamie had expected life alone on the run to be challenging, but never had she expected bullets to be grazing her skin, or an attractive bounty hunter to be deciding what to do with her. He was comforting, with his quiet voice and his gentle touch. If she let them, thousands of thoughts could easily overwhelm—

No. She closed her eyes for a few seconds and shook her head. He wasn't her friend or a possible date. He was with her only because he wanted to collect the money he'd get for bringing her in to the authorities.

Still, trusting him was a risk, but at the moment, she had no choice. Her ability to make sound decisions in such danger had grown weaker with each day.

"Lil, I need to talk to Parker." Zack stood before her with his phone stuck to his ear, his tone tense, his gaze scanning their surroundings. Seconds ticked by. "Hey, listen…Yes, I know, but I need you to stop for a minute. I need one of you to come pick me up on the Ponahochet side of Champlain Park…No, there's no time to explain. You just need to make it as fast as you can… Parker, please. It's important." With a glance her way, he added, "And bring the first-aid kit."

He got off the phone and tucked it into his pocket. "They'll be here soon."

With a push off the bench, she got to her feet and slung the backpack over her shoulder.

Zack held his hand out toward her waist. "Where are you going?"

She shook her head. "I can't risk you getting into trouble for me."

He rolled his eyes. "You just saved my life. I'm thinking I still owe *you*."

"I can't go to jail, either."

"What exactly do you think your sister's husband has done that makes him such a menace?" A hint of disbelief still threaded through his expression.

*He killed my sister.* She lowered her gaze to the bloodied sleeve. "Too much."

"Those guys we just ran into might be deputies, as you say, but they aren't on my side of the justice fence. Clearly, you're in over your head. Going into a state police station might be best."

"No." She scanned the park. "I've made my decision. I'm not going." She took a few steps in the direction of the park entrance. Two little girls giggled from their upside-down positions on the monkey bars, one wobbling back and forth, the other with big pigtails dangling next to her ears.

Memories rushed forward to a time when she and Erin had been cared for, loved, cherished. Thoughts of the last time she and Erin had brought Charlotte for a playdate sprang to mind, as well. That day, Erin had insisted Drew needed her to bring him back to God. And for doing her duty as a child of God, Drew had killed her.

"Where will you go?" Zack's voice brought her back to the present. "Where you have the kid stashed? You can't go back to the camping area I just found you in. Or your apartment across town. If the goon squad found you once, they'll find you again. Are you planning to fight the next round while you're less than one hundred percent?"

She stepped around him. But he was right. At the moment, depending on him might not be the wisest choice, but she had no one else. Not even God would give her a break.

When she turned back, Zack stood there, his eyes pleading for her trust. Several moments filled with tension ticked by. "Jamie, let me help you figure out what's next."

Her head grew dizzy, but from the loss of blood, the adrenaline-charged events or as a result of his offer to help, she couldn't be sure. Could she afford to accept his assistance?

Could she afford not to?

# TWO

"Come on." Zack waved her toward his side of the bench. As the children continued to laugh, he watched them play.

Such an odd man. With his taut muscle and healthy body, Zack could definitely force her to do what he wanted. Instead, he walked away, allowing her to feel like she was choosing to stay with him. Truthfully, she wasn't sure how to interpret his behavior.

She retreated to the bench, lowered her backpack and sat beside him. The reality was she needed another level head to decipher all that had happened, someone not directly involved. She also needed to rest—her arm, her mind, her heart. Running took its toll and today it felt like she was on the verge of being completely defeated.

A red SUV hurried through the gates on the other side of the park. "They're here." Zack took hold of her good arm and guided her toward the road. As the vehicle screeched to a halt in front of them, the side door slid open. A different woman than the one at the internet café hunched down and kept her hand on the ceiling grip. She reached out to Jamie with her other hand.

"Go ahead," Zack said quietly.

She struggled to climb into the vehicle. Why did her legs feel like cooked noodles?

"Sit there," the woman ordered as she pointed to the seat behind the driver. A long ponytail of dark chocolate-colored hair waved behind her.

As Zack hopped in and closed the door behind him, the woman moved to the back of the vehicle. Jamie pushed her backpack between her seat and the door and glanced around. Two men sat in the front, one with hair as dark as Zack's but a bit longer and one with shorter, dark brown hair. The one with the long hair sat cramped in the front passenger seat.

Once the vehicle headed out of the park, the woman grabbed something from the floor. "Which one of you needs the first-aid kit?"

"She does." Zack pointed. "Give it here."

The woman handed it over.

"What've you gotten yourself into now?" The driver's sharp tone sliced into Jamie's already frayed nerves.

"We ran into some trouble." Zack fished through the kit for items to clean and bandage her arm.

"Obviously." The guy in the passenger seat glared their way.

"Do we need to go to the ER?" The driver glanced into the rearview mirror.

"No," she and Zack answered simultaneously. Emergency rooms were required to contact police about shootings. If there was any question about a bullet singeing her skin, Jamie would be forced to kiss her freedom and her chance of investigating her brother-in-law goodbye.

If she hadn't already.

The two men in the front exchanged looks, then the passenger and the woman did. A thousand ideas about what kind of people they were raced through Jamie's head, enough to start a headache. Three more people who may or may not believe her. Three more people who could potentially ruin her rush toward her next goal— stopping by Mrs. Cecily's house. She should've tried to run while she and Zack waited in the park. On a regular day, she would have, but being around Zack messed with her head.

Everyone was silent as they traveled through the narrow roads of the city. His fingers were gentle as Zack began tending to her wound.

Questions burned inside the people around her, she was sure. The passenger watched Zack work. From the corner of her eye, she could see the woman behind them sitting forward with her hands on the backs of their seats. The driver stole a glance through the rearview mirror whenever he could.

The SUV slowed and turned into an almost deserted parking lot. The big neon letters of a grocery store's name threatened to fall completely off the billboard. A shopping cart rolled on its own across the lopsided pavement. Out the front window, traffic traveled like normal.

To the rest of the world, it didn't matter that someone had shot in her direction a little over an hour ago. She pressed her thumb pad against her lips and willed the moisture to stay away from her eyes. Drew and his cronies had forced enough tears out of her.

"What now?" she dared to ask. But she needed to know so she could plan *her* next step.

Once he'd set the car in Park, the driver turned. His gaze shifted from her to Zack. "Little brother, you finish up, then come outside with us."

He, the passenger and the woman behind her all exited the vehicle, then slammed the doors shut. Tension swirled with anxiety inside her. As the others gathered on the sidewalk by the hood of the vehicle, Zack said nothing. Their mumbling voices drifted through the cracked open window, but she couldn't decipher their conversation. Too often, they glanced inside the SUV.

Zack brushed some salve on her wound before taping a bandage over it. "How's it feeling now?"

She cupped her fingers around the bandage. "It's not on fire anymore."

Zack pressed his palm over her hand. "Good."

For several seconds, they locked gazes. Longing swarmed through her belly, but for what she couldn't be sure. Maybe just for the tenderness he offered. "For someone so tough and intimidating, you have gentle hands."

As he replaced items in the kit, he chuckled. "I can't remember the last time anyone called me gentle."

"Thank you."

He set the kit on the floor. "Are you kidding? Thank *you*."

With a quick glance back out the windshield, she caught the driver pointing inside to them. "Your driver doesn't like me much."

Zack leaned closer until his shoulder brushed against hers and his scent surrounded her head. "That's Kyle, my oldest brother. He's the one with the shrewd head on his shoulders."

"And the others?"

"Parker, my other brother who's not as obstinate as Kyle, and Jessa, our only female partner. Parker and my sister, the woman you fought the other day, are twins."

"What do you think they're talking about out there?" She nudged her chin toward them.

"Us." He sat staring through the window with his lips pressed together. "Sit tight."

He slid the door open, hopped out, then closed it again. The other three glanced in his direction as he approached. Jamie imagined muscles tensing as calm words morphed into jerked motions. Several times Kyle, the driver, pointed toward her again.

Trusting the very people trained to turn her in? A complete mistake.

She leaned back against the seat and closed her eyes. No more did she want to see accusing glares or fingers.

A few minutes later, the doors to the SUV opened. As the bounty hunting team reentered the vehicle, Jamie didn't ask any questions. Truthfully, all the answers they could possibly give scared her and showing fear left her powerless. She had to remain strong or she'd never be able to do right by her sister.

Everyone took their seats again. Kyle glanced at her through the rearview mirror. "Jamie, tell us why those guys were shooting at you."

Her dry mouth stalled. She looked toward Zack. How much should she share?

"Zack's told us his version, but we want to hear it from you, too," Parker, the passenger, added with a bit of kindness in his voice.

She fingered her necklace, the cross her sister had given her in hopes of assisting Jamie's return to God. But God had given up on her.

After taking a deep breath, she retold the public events of her life starting from the day she lost her sister.

Jessa leaned forward. "I don't get it, though. Why shoot at you? If they killed you, you wouldn't be able to lead them to your niece."

"They weren't shooting at me." Jamie made a point to meet the gaze of each person in the vehicle.

Parker's eyes widened for a fleeting second, then he faced the front window. Kyle glanced back to the road. Jessa chewed on her thumbnail.

"All right. We've got to go." Kyle started the vehicle and pulled into the busy traffic.

"Kyle, maybe—" Parker began.

"It doesn't change anything." Kyle shook his head.

Jamie stared out her window with her hands in her lap. Cars rolled along the road, a young couple laughed as they leaned against each other and walked down the sidewalk, a van sat in front of a brownstone with movers unloading furniture. These were normal lives. Would she ever get her chance to participate again?

Probably not, and after failing her sister, Jamie didn't deserve one.

The vehicle turned into a parking lot under a set of beautiful oak trees. The small, rustic building Drew used as his legal headquarters sat with a hill as a backdrop... and two sheriff's vehicles were parked by the entrance to Ponahochet County Sheriff's Office. Jamie gripped the edge of the armrests. "What are you doing?"

No one said a word. None of the others dared to look in her direction.

"Zack?" Her voice held a desperation she couldn't hide.

Kyle parked next to a sheriff's car.

Zack reached for her but must've thought better of it. Instead, he closed his fingers in a loose fist. "We have to turn you in."

*Oh, no, no, no.* A whirlwind of emotions shot through

Jamie. Her feet readied for flight. "You can't drop me off. Not here."

"We have to." The side door rolled open. From somewhere along the parking lot, birds chirped a happy tune. Other vehicles crunched gravel as they wandered toward the shopping mall down the other end of the block.

Zack hopped out of the SUV. "Come on."

But she didn't move. Instead, she scanned the others in the vehicle. Once, twice she opened her mouth, but the plea she held in her throat wouldn't mean a thing to these people. Besides, begging wasn't her style.

"Jamie."

She climbed out. Zack wrapped his long, firm fingers around her wrist and guided her toward the front doors. With each step closer, panic itched inside her. "Zack, please don't do this."

Even if she managed to break free of his hold, she wouldn't get far before he grabbed her. Or one of his family members would.

"I have to. It's my job."

"After I saved your life, this is the way you're choosing to treat me?" Groveling? Um, what had she just reminded herself about begging?

"You have a warrant out on you and I'm still a bounty hunter. Turning you in is the right decision."

"Who are you trying to convince? Me or yourself?" She stopped them both outside the glass entryway. His fingers pinched the skin of her wrist as she tried to break free.

"Jamie, please don't make this harder than it already is."

"From the way you listened, the way you took care of me, I thought you believed in the truth." And Charlotte.

If Jamie didn't return to her friend's house, would Greta be able to keep the little girl safe? Would Drew eventually find them? And if Erin had gathered any evidence of Drew's drug business, would Mrs. Cecily be able to help prove Drew was a bad sheriff?

"I promise we'll do whatever we can to help you when you go to court and afterward. We'll even check on your niece when she goes back with her father, so he knows someone is paying attention." He reached for the door handle.

"You don't understand. If you leave me here, Drew's won and I'll never be able to prove he's responsible for my sister's death." Or how dangerous he was even for his own community.

She pressed her fingers to his forearm. When he turned to her, regret drifted through his face. "Zack, please."

For a long moment, he stared at her, as though he still wrestled with his decision. "I'm sorry."

She nodded and straightened her spine. "I should've known I couldn't trust you." She grabbed the handle, pulled the door open and stepped through.

Deputy George Linden's droning laugh sailed across the room. He stood with his hands on the secretary's shoulders, sharing a joke or comment she also found funny.

Jamie's feet stalled. George was bad enough, but was Drew here? How much worse could her situation get? What did Zack see when he looked at George, Drew's best friend? A stocky man wearing the standard brown deputy uniform. A colleague, someone to follow the law like he did. She wished she had some way to reveal

George's blackened heart to the bounty hunter. Maybe then he'd believe her.

Why couldn't God let *anyone* believe her that Drew was bad news?

Zack nudged her forward across the lobby. George and the woman looked up. A mournful tune leaked out of a nearby radio.

The deputy rolled his shoulders back. "Jamie Carter." George wandered around her, as if studying a piece of meat and wondering whether to keep it or throw it away. When he turned to face Zack, he wore one of his politician smiles. "I'm Deputy Linden."

Zack hesitated but then shook the other man's hand. "Zack Owen of Second Chance Bail Bonds."

"You're not from around here."

"No, sir. We work in Gilliam, outside of Warwick."

George gripped his belt buckle. The muscles of his arms strained the fabric of his uniform shirt. "We've been hunting this one for a while now. I know the sheriff will appreciate you bringing her in."

"I can call him," the secretary offered.

"Not necessary. I'll be talking to him later." He turned his attention to Zack. "The sheriff's out of town at a conference, but he's due home tomorrow morning."

Jamie relaxed her fingers out of tight fists. She'd have a bit of time to come up with a plan. And to delay the wrath of her brother-in-law.

George narrowed his gaze on her, a whirlwind of threats hidden behind his dark eyes.

She flinched.

"Sheriff Timmins is so worried about his kid. And her."

"*Worried* isn't the word I'd use," she said under her breath.

"We've told you there's no way out of this, Jamie." George's hand clamped down on her shoulder, the pressure tight. As he spoke, his eyes settled on her arm. "Drew's willing to work with you to find a peaceful solution to you stealing your niece, but you've got to make the effort to be civil."

She kept her mouth shut. Arguing with him would only make her head ache and make him feisty.

George grabbed Jamie's arm, right above her wound. On purpose, she was sure. She gritted her teeth but refused to cry out. "Mr. Owen, Sharon will get you all set up with the proper paperwork you'll need to sign."

After a skeptical glance in Jamie's direction, Zack walked to the counter. Sharon's oversize earrings jingled as she shoved her hand through her shoulder-length, straw-like hair.

While inching closer to her ear, George clenched her wounded skin. Tight. The pain raced up to her brain and threatened to drop her to the floor. "If I call Drew now, he might cut his trip short. Then your arm injury will be the least of your worries." The words of his threat cut right through her bravado. The fight in her disappeared a little more with each second.

As he snickered, he moved his hand to her shoulder, his fingers pinching her skin at the back of her neck. "You may think you're tough now, but we'll get what we want and, in the end, you'll be begging for us to kill you."

Jamie's gaze darted across the room. Zack stared in their direction. Was he having second thoughts?

*Please don't leave me.*

"Sir, I've got one more paper for you to fill out." The secretary waved a single page in front of Zack. He returned his attention to his duty.

George guided Jamie toward the thigh-high gate along the counter.

"We're just about set here, Deputy." Sharon shuffled the papers together and slid them into a manila folder.

George faced Zack and held his hand out. "Thank you, Mr. Owen, for bringing her in."

Zack knocked his knuckles on the counter. "You know what? Can I speak with her for one more minute? I want to clarify some information she gave me earlier…about another fugitive."

Optimism sparked within her.

The deputy shook his head. "No, I'm sorry. I need to get her fingerprinted and processed."

The men stood facing each other. They were at an impasse.

Jamie clenched her fists. *Don't give up on me, Zack.*

But the plea remained locked in her mind. The bounty hunter nodded. "All right. You guys have a good night."

With each step Zack took toward the exit, one more shard of hope died inside Jamie.

"Let's go make a phone call." George shoved her down the hallway toward the back of the building.

Once again, Jamie was on her own in a battle she barely knew how to fight.

The pursuit of Jamie Carter was over. All tied up in a neat little bow. After one final look into the hallway, Zack strolled out of the building. But the gnawing in his gut refused to disappear. The deputy hadn't even asked about the blood on her shirt. And the fear in her eyes… What if Jamie was telling the truth about Linden and her brother-in-law? If so, he'd just handed her over like a used ten-dollar bill. But his brothers had made the decision to bring her to *this* sheriff's station. He knew they were legally required to do so.

Then why did he feel guilty for doing his job?

He squinted against the bright sunlight while he walked back to his brother's vehicle. Once he'd climbed in, Jessa asked, "All set?"

"Yup." As he settled in his seat and closed the door, he stared out the window. Kyle rejoined the traffic line.

"It was the right thing to do, Zack."

He said nothing. Yeah, from a professional point of view, Kyle was right.

But the fear in her sparkling eyes...

Parker twisted around in his seat. "We can have Lily check up on her if you want."

"Yeah, okay," he answered half-heartedly. He should shove Jamie out of his mind. Yes, he cared, but it was because of his love for the law. Her impassioned pleas and the way the fire fizzled within her beautiful expression when he'd signed her over to the deputy had absolutely no effect on him. *Let her go.*

The uncomfortable feeling in Zack's gut refused to disappear through the night. Instead, a thread of guilt spun around and around until he could think of nothing else but Jamie—her pretty eyes, her brown hair drifting in the wind, her courage. He hadn't heard her laugh yet, but maybe it would be contagious.

The next day, he walked through the front door to work. Lily sat behind her desk, wiggling in her chair to some oldies song. "Morning, Zack."

"Hey." Other than his sister's music floating from the ancient radio she'd kept from Dad, no sounds filled the room. He hung up the keys on the key rack behind Lil's desk. "Where is everybody?"

"They went out on an early run." Lil swiveled in her chair to the far end of her counter and grabbed a pile of folders. "Here." She held them out to him. "Kyle said you'd know what to do with these."

Pitch them in the garbage? "Great." Exactly what he wanted to do. He snatched the busywork out of his sister's hands.

Lil dropped her chin in her palm and a mischievous grin spread across her face. "Want to go on another run together?"

"Not after the flak I got from Kyle and Parker for taking you along the other day." It's why he'd left her at the office yesterday when he went after Jamie.

"Come on." She held up her clipboard. "I put together a list of some skips who would be safe enough. I promise I'll follow all your directions."

He raised his eyebrows. "Like you did at the café? No thanks."

Resigned to working in the office again, he headed for his desk.

All four of them worked in one messy room not far behind Lily. Well, the side he and Kyle occupied had neat piles and dust-free surfaces. Parker and Jessa's side looked like a tornado blew through it. Folders piled up, loose pages scattered across desks, crumpled papers next to the trash bin, probably from Parker's pathetic attempts to score a basket.

Tornado. Blizzard. Hurricane. Raging storms destined to wreak havoc on his world.

Jamie Carter.

He stopped in front of his desk and leaned his head

back. Why wouldn't the woman leave his brain alone? *God, what are you doing to me?*

"Lil," he began as he sat in his chair. "Can you call the Ponahochet County Sheriff's Office and make sure Jamie Carter's been transferred to see the magistrate?"

"Got it."

He tapped the folders repeatedly on the edge of the desk. He'd get busy with the boring paperwork he had to cover when he had an answer about Jamie. Once the music grew quiet, Lil's voice took on an official tone for the call.

A few minutes later, she hung up. "She's still with Ponahochet Sheriff's Office." Her voice sailed in from the lobby.

He slid the files onto the desk. The music resumed.

Realistically there could be a bunch of reasons Jamie hadn't been transferred. "Not my problem."

When Zack first started out in the family business, he'd had a steady girlfriend who developed multiple sclerosis. Because he was so worried about her, he neglected his duty on a fugitive hunt and as a result, an innocent gas station cashier got hurt. Kyle had let him have it, with threats of probation and even firing. In the time since, Zack had been successful in keeping emotion of any kind out of his business.

Until Jamie.

He shook his head and opened the top folder. "Think with practical sense, not sappy feelings." *Stay out of it.*

But the deputy had said Timmins would be back from his conference this morning. Maybe the second in command had decided to keep his prisoner for the sheriff's return.

Zack could drive to Ponahochet to check on Jamie,

make sure her sister's husband and his deputy hadn't done anything to hurt her. No harm in that, right?

Lily popped into his line of sight and leaned against the doorjamb with her arms crossed. "What are you going to do?"

"What do you mean?" He shifted his chair closer to the desk, avoided her gaze.

"Don't play dumb, Z. We both know the woman's story affected you."

Picking up a pen, he shook his head. "No, you've got—"

"Don't try to deny it. I'm older and wiser. Besides, you're easy to read."

"What's the point? I can't do anything to change her situation. She has to face the consequences of her actions." He flipped through the pages in front of him. "Besides, it's none of my business."

"There's no harm in showing a little compassion. The woman's probably scared about what she's facing. You could help her through it, explain the process, answer any questions, maybe help her little niece."

Several moments ticked by. Zack couldn't be *that guy*, not even for *this woman*. Following through with any of Lily's suggestions would make him too invested in Jamie. He'd been invested in his former girlfriend and had caused an amazing amount of pain as a result for everyone involved. Zack couldn't go through that again.

On the other hand, Jamie could use a friend, and hadn't he promised to help strangers in need? He rubbed his eyes.

Lily chucked his truck keys to him. "Go check on her. Then you'll be able to concentrate on your paperwork afterward. I promise I won't say a thing to the others."

Without giving him a chance to argue anymore, she wandered back to her desk.

He blew out a heavy breath. Too many questions surrounded the attractive teacher with no definitive answers. He gripped the keys tighter. Heading to Ponahochet could only stir up a load of trouble. But if he did nothing and an innocent woman got hurt again, would he ever be able to forgive himself?

His decision didn't really hold so much weight. Either way something would go wrong. Might as well follow his conscience, just this time.

Zack marched through the doors of the Ponahochet County Sheriff's Office with a folder of fake rebonding forms in his hand. He didn't like the idea of using them, but he'd planned ahead in case he needed to remove Jamie from a dangerous situation. At once, the stink of burned popcorn surrounded him. Sappy love songs played through a speaker somewhere above him.

Sharon sat in her same spot as his first visit, behind the counter, this time with her hand stuck in a bowl full of the snack food. "Morning, Mr. Owen." She moved her glasses to the edge of her nose. "What can I do for you?"

"Morning." Zack set his arms on the counter. "Is the sheriff or Deputy Linden in?"

"Nope. Deputy Linden's off to pick the sheriff up at the airport."

Relief spread through him with the news. Both men missing from the office? One less difficulty. All that was left was his conscience. "I need to take Ms. Carter with me."

Sharon stopped mid-chew. "What?"

"She's been rebonded out of Stenness County. I didn't find out until I got to the office this morning."

She tapped her pen against her chin. "I don't know. I'll have to clear it with the deputy first."

*God, forgive me.* "I've got the forms." He pushed the folder toward her, leaned a little closer and grinned. "I messed up bringing her here yesterday. I need your help fixing it, Sharon. Please tell me I can count on you." For added measure, he also gave her a wink.

A smile emerged as her cheeks reddened. "Well…" She pulled the folder to her desk and glanced over the paperwork. When she stood, she grabbed a set of keys hanging by the hallway and waved him along. "Come on, then."

He followed her down the hallway. On the left, two empty cells flanked another hallway with several other doors. Probably restrooms, the processing room, maybe a break room. To his right were two more cells. He and Sharon stopped in front of the second one.

"Ms. Carter, you've got company." Jingling the keys, Sharon continued, "Sweetie, come on up here."

Zack scanned Jamie's jail cell. A hard, metal bed, if you could call it that, hung from the far wall. No chair, no blanket, no pillow. A barred window allowed in little light.

Jamie sat diagonally away from him with her knees pulled up to her chest and her head down. Yikes. He'd thought she looked small and fragile before.

"Leave me alone," she mumbled.

"Let's go, Jamie. You're being rebonded." Would his voice bring her comfort or more suspicion?

She lifted her head slowly. Wide eyes met his gaze as her shoulders drooped. The receptionist turned the key and pulled the cell door open. "I'll finish up the paperwork."

"Thank you." Zack shifted into the tiny room.

Sharon nodded, then disappeared toward the lobby.

"What are you doing here?" Jamie hadn't moved from her spot. "And what's this about rebonding?" She still wore the cropped jeans she'd worn when he picked her up, but the T-shirt was different. And yet, there were specks of red on the sleeve over her injury.

"I…" *Was concerned?* No, he wouldn't want her to get the wrong idea about his visit. He was here to make sure the sheriff's office followed the law, not because he longed for her. Zack Owen refused to long for any woman.

Yet, Jamie had already found a way to tuck herself somewhere inside him.

He closed the distance between them and crouched before her. "I just told Sharon about you being rebonded so I could get you out of here."

Hope swam in her hazel eyes. "You mean you believe me now?"

"I don't know what I believe." He saw it then, a dark purple mark around the corner of her eye. His gut clenched as he reached forward. His fingertips carefully brushed the silky strands of her hair away from the bruise so he could examine it more closely. "Did Linden do this?"

She flinched. "I told you he was bad news. He started the interrogation yesterday, asking me where my niece, Charlotte, is and I refused to turn her over. He'll be back with Drew soon and the two of them will push me even harder." Her piercing gaze hit him, as though he were the cause of her newest bruise.

Wasn't he?

He glanced toward the front of the building even though Linden wasn't there. The lawman who was supposed to protect people. The deputy who hadn't followed through with his duty.

Closing his fist, Zack stood. Once he occupied the doorway, he called out, "Sharon?"

"Yes?" The older woman moved into his line of vision but remained by her desk area.

"How'd Ms. Carter get hurt?"

"Deputy Linden said she fell against the bed when she was struggling to get away from him."

"You didn't see it happen?"

"No, I'd already left for the day." She returned to her seat and began singing off-key to the tune on the radio.

Zack turned his attention back to Jamie. The urge to fold his arms around her almost overwhelmed him. She needed protection, an ally.

"So, do you believe my story now?"

Unfortunately, he did believe her, and with the acknowledgment, a huge weight dropped onto his shoulders. If Zack walked away, the woman, and possibly a helpless child, would suffer. Staying with Jamie would put him in the direct line of fire. Either decision would bring a truckload of trouble.

Guilt would claw at him if he left her. His siblings might explode if he didn't.

Once again, his gaze shifted from Jamie to the lobby, then back to Jamie. Adrenaline pumped through him. He folded and unfolded his fingers.

Walk away…be consumed with guilt.

Take another step for Jamie…possibly put her in more danger.

*Possibly.*

As a child of God, he had no choice. "Come on." He stalked toward her, took her hands and pulled her to her feet. "Hopefully we'll get out of here before Linden and your brother-in-law get back." He grabbed his handcuffs from his belt and clamped them on her wrists.

"Zack, are you sure?"

No, he wasn't. He pulled her close enough to see the mix of colors in her eyes. "Please trust me."

She stared at him with such vulnerability, and yet *weak* wasn't a word he'd ever use to describe this woman he barely knew.

After what felt like forever, she nodded. With her consent, he urged her into the hallway. No turning back now.

# THREE

Jamie's brain swirled with a ton of thoughts. She'd trusted Zack yesterday and landed in a jail cell. Why should she put her faith in him now?

On the other hand, leaving with this man had to be better than facing Drew when George brought him back from the airport.

Her body filled with nervous energy as they reached the lobby. Zack held the swing gate for her to pass through, then shifted to the counter without ever letting go of Jamie's uninjured arm.

Sharon's fingers flew over the computer keyboard, then the printer kicked on. "Almost ready."

"You are a lifesaver. I'm already in so much trouble with my coworkers about this mix-up. I can't tell you how much I appreciate your cooperation." A charming smile stretched across his lips.

A handsome face, an easygoing personality—he had the characteristics of all Hollywood's leading men combined. The sparkle in his eye even managed to bump a few butterflies to life in Jamie's own stomach. With him, she could easily forget she was a wanted criminal and just focus on being…a woman.

But he was still dangerous on so many levels. She had to stay focused on bringing Drew down. That was all that mattered. Getting caught up in her romantic thoughts about a man she only met a few days ago would not help her right the wrong she'd committed by ignoring her sister's final call for help.

Sharon grabbed papers off the printer, stuck them in a folder and held it out. "All set. I'll let the sheriff know what happened."

"Thanks so much. You've come to my rescue." His words and his stature both exuded confidence. He pushed off the counter, then winked at the older woman.

Her smile widened. "Oh, go on." She waved him away.

"Yes, ma'am." Quickly he urged Jamie out the front door. The sunshine blinded her. When she lifted her hands to shield her eyes, Zack wrapped his arm around her shoulders. "This way."

"You're really letting me escape?" It couldn't be this easy. He'd want something for his kindness. Most men did.

"No, but I'm not letting you get sacrificed, either." He opened the passenger-side door of a white pickup. "Hop in."

Jamie gathered her nerves and lifted her chin. "Can you at least take these off?" She jingled the metal bracelets still on her wrists.

"We need to get out of here before your brother-in-law and his driver show up or one of his other deputies who hates you gets here. Get in the truck."

She slid a glance along the road, then met Zack's gaze. He waited for her to comply. Impatience caused his fingers to tap against the door frame. Yes, the unknown she'd face with Zack unnerved her. But she'd experienced the dangerous road with George and she knew how vicious Drew could be. Right now, going with Zack was the best decision for her.

\* \* \*

Zack pulled into the parking lot of the plaza that housed Second Chance Bail Bonds, turned off the engine and stared at the back door of the office. Jamie sat next to him, as silent as she'd been since he'd unlocked her handcuffs shortly after leaving Timmins's office. He folded his fingers into a tight fist.

Jamie fidgeted and glanced out of the windows. "Why are we here?"

Taking her away from the abusive sheriff's department had been a good moral decision. Now he needed his brothers to brainstorm the next move. He already had one idea—drop her off at the state police station—but in his gut, he felt he needed to support her. It seemed no one else wanted to believe her. "I need an objective opinion." He pulled the door handle. "Come on."

"Wait." Cool, soft fingers settled on his forearm. As a chill wrestled through his arm, Zack turned to her. "Are you sure this is a good idea?"

There was the vulnerability again, leaking out of her soft eyes. He cupped his hand around her cheek and brushed his thumb beneath the bruise by her eye. "Truthfully? No, but at the moment we don't have another choice. I'm used to being one of the good guys and you're running out of places to hide."

Jamie tilted her head into his hand and closed her eyes, as though surrendering some power to him. The tiny bit of trust tugged on his heartstrings.

But he couldn't get wrapped up in her situation, in her. He released her and exited the vehicle. As she joined him by the back door, he shoved his truck keys into his front pocket.

"Wait. Where's my backpack?" she asked.

"What are you talking about?"

"I left it in the SUV yesterday."

He shook his head. "I don't think it's there. No one brought it into the office. Maybe you left it in the park."

"No." She stalked toward the red vehicle with him right behind. "I stuffed it between my seat and the door. I couldn't bring it into George and Drew's office. You were the lesser of two evils."

Zack pulled the vehicle's door open. The plaid backpack fell to the ground.

Jamie caught it. "Thank you," she whispered as she clutched the bag with both arms. Was she speaking to him or to God? "Okay, I'm ready."

Once they entered the back door of the office, Jamie slowed and turned to him. Lily's radio played from the lobby. Zack wrapped one arm around Jamie's back. Although touching her wasn't necessary to reassure her, he wanted to. "It's okay." After guiding her farther into the building, he stopped by the conference room. "Wait in here." Again, her gaze met his with a thousand questions he couldn't answer. "Go on. I'll be right back."

With his partner in crime stowed away, he continued walking to the front of the building. His sister sat dancing at her desk with a stack of folders in front of her. "Hey, Lil." From the couch, Jessa lowered her magazine. "Jessa."

Lily glanced in his direction. "Everything work out?" she whispered.

"Not exactly." He passed behind her and stopped in the doorway of the office he shared with the others. His brothers sat at their desks, Parker doing some paperwork and Kyle typing on his computer.

"How are those reports comin'?" Kyle didn't glance Zack's way or stop typing.

*Here goes nothing.* "Guys, I did something stupid."

Lily's chair creaked, then she popped up and stood beside him.

"Yeah, Lily already told us you went back to Pona-hochet to check on the woman from yesterday." Parker flipped a folder closed. "It's okay."

"I didn't just go back to check on her."

Kyle's fingers hung just above the computer keys. "What do you mean?"

*I broke the law I've been sworn to protect.*

Too many seconds ticked by with only the chorus of a classic rock tune floating through the room. "Zack, what did you do?" Kyle crossed his arms on the edge of the desk.

"Come see." He waved them out of the room. Parker and Kyle practically jumped from their seats and followed Lily and him.

Jessa joined them, too. "What are we doing?"

Zack guided them to the conference room and stepped through the doorway. On the far side, with her back to the door and the backpack over her shoulder, stood Jamie. She whirled around with her chin held high. Sunlight draped over her shoulders, as though highlighting her strength and confidence. Pride filled him and he couldn't help but smile.

"Uh-oh," Lil said at the same moment as Jessa.

Parker asked, "What is she doing here?"

Right. She wasn't the girlfriend he was introducing to his family. She was a wanted criminal. "I had to get her out. She was absolutely terrified."

She propped her hands on her hips. "I wouldn't say *terrified.*"

Kyle grabbed the door handle and pinned Jamie with his signature death stare. "Don't move from this room," he ordered before pulling the door shut. "Zack, are you insane? You broke the woman out of jail. Technically, we could escort you to the sheriff's office right alongside her."

Kyle didn't tell him anything he hadn't already thought about on his own. "I know, but, guys, she has a black eye. I know for a fact none of us gave it to her yesterday, so it had to be the deputy."

"What was his explanation?" Lily moved back to her desk.

"He wasn't there. Just the secretary."

"She let you walk out together?" Parker asked. Jessa kept quiet and reclaimed her spot on the couch. She was the smart one. She almost always kept her mouth closed when any of the siblings argued.

"Not exactly." Zack leaned his head to one side.

"Which means what…*exactly*?" Kyle matched his gaze.

He shrugged. "I sold her a story."

Parker banged his forehead against the doorjamb. Kyle massaged his temples, mumbling a prayer no doubt. Jessa whistled as she flipped another page of her magazine.

Zack pressed his lips together. Somehow this conversation wasn't happening the way he'd practiced it in his head. "Guys, I know I messed up a little, but—"

Kyle snickered. "No, you messed up a lot."

"You're a fool to risk your career for a woman who may or may not be lying to you." Parker crossed his arms.

"Are you attracted to her?" Kyle asked. "Is that why you're acting stupid? 'Cause I can tell you now—"

"That's gotta be it," Parker added.

"No, guys. You know I'm not interested in a relationship with anyone." Too many emotions created too much vulnerability, which could lead to too much pain for him, for a woman or for an innocent. "It's just…" Something he didn't know how to put in words.

"You're not thinking, Z. Do you realize…"

Kyle's words morphed into mumbles Zack had no desire to hear. How he felt about Jamie didn't matter. Even if he wanted to hear her laugh or see her give him a genuine smile, he had to focus on getting her to safety. "No, listen, Kyle. I brought her here to keep her safe from crooked authorities. It's a sound business decision. I brought her to you and Parker because we need to know what we can do next." Zack walked to the center of the lobby.

Kyle rubbed his forehead, then began pacing across the room. "I don't know, Zack. I've been at this job longer, but you're the best bounty hunter I've seen. When you're on the hunt, you're steady, cool, even shrewd. You've got good instincts, but I don't know where your head is right now."

"Which is why I came to you."

"Guys, let's focus on the immediate problem." Parker held his hands out, one to each of them.

"She may not be telling me the whole truth, but something's definitely not right, and we can't let a woman suffer physical pain if we can help it," Zack said.

Silence crept up, stopped only by the crick-crack of the air conditioner coming on.

"She almost took a bullet for me. I owe her."

His older brothers, the men who had trained him in the business, who had watched out for him and gotten him out of countless rounds of trouble as a kid, both stared him down.

"Okay, so I messed up." He glanced behind him to the conference room door. Could Jamie hear him defending her? Maybe it would help her trust him enough for her to share all her hidden secrets. Her *case* hidden secrets, not her personal ones. "Should we take her to the state police and turn her in?"

"Yes," Kyle, Parker and even Jessa said at the same moment.

"Then you better get going." Lily pointed outside. "A sheriff's car is pulling into the parking lot as we speak."

"Timmins is here? Already?" Zack and his brothers turned to face the doorway. Jessa peeked through the blinds.

"You had to know this would be his first stop." Parker grabbed one of their fugitive folders and held it open next to Lily, as though they had been discussing a case. Jessa sat back against the couch.

"Yeah, but I thought we'd have a plan by then and Jamie and I would be gone."

Kyle shoved Zack down the hall. "Hide her out back, then get your behind in here."

A dark-haired man, taller and thinner than Deputy Linden, exited his vehicle. A few steps closer to tearing apart Zack's lies.

"Move, Zack," Parker urged.

Zack rushed to the conference room and waved Jamie toward him. "We've got to go."

"Why?" She maneuvered around the furniture. "What's wrong?"

"Later." When she was close enough, he set his hands on her waist and pushed her toward the back door. "Go."

Sunlight temporarily blinded him, but he kept going. He opened his truck's tailgate. "Take the blanket and whatever else you can find to cover yourself and don't move until I come out for you."

"What's happening?" Worry lined her tired features.

"Do what I tell you," he snapped.

For a few seconds she stared at him, looking as vulnerable as he felt. "Jamie." He grabbed her arm and urged her into the truck.

This time she did as he instructed. While she grabbed the blanket and pulled it over her, he closed the truck tailgate as quietly as he could.

After taking a deep breath, he reentered the building. Sharp threats charged from the front of the office. "I demand you tell me where they are."

For good measure, Zack slipped into the bathroom to flush the toilet before walking into the front room.

Parker pointed to him. "There's our brother."

Zack made a quick evaluation of the new guy—taller than the deputy by a couple inches; not as bulky in the chest but still well-built. He definitely spent time in the gym. When he wasn't beating up on helpless women. "You must be Sheriff Timmins."

The sheriff nodded once. "I hear you found my sister-in-law. Thank you. We've been worried. But now I need her back. Where is she?"

"How would I know?" Zack asked.

"Don't play dumb with me. Sharon told my deputy and me you took Jamie this morning." The sheriff drilled his gaze into Zack. "Something about her being rebonded."

*God, forgive me for lying.* "I turned her in at Stenness County Sheriff's Department like I told your secretary."

"Yet she wasn't there when I called to verify." Timmins planted his hands on his hips. "So where is she?"

"Like I said, I don't know. Instead of harassing me, why don't you go downtown and find her yourself? I know you probably can't wait to get your hands on her again."

Timmins motioned Zack closer as he inched forward. "Why don't you come over here and say that?"

Kyle shifted to Zack's left, Parker to his right. "You don't want to do anything stupid, Sheriff," Parker warned.

Timmins glanced at each of them. "You want to talk about dumb? I could have you out of business in three seconds flat if I wanted, yet you insist on helping a woman you know nothing about."

"And I could have you investigated for sending goons to shoot at her and me." The men at the campsite hadn't worn uniforms or flashed badges, but Zack was sure they came on Timmins's orders. "Shoot first and ask questions later. Is that the way you run your office, Sheriff?"

"I'm sorry if you feel you got caught in the cross fire, but the men thought you were helping my sister-in-law to escape and evade us."

Lily piped up, "He's a bounty hunter. He was trying to bring the woman in peacefully."

Timmins glared at Lil. Zack wasn't used to seeing his big sister back down, but Lil's eyes widened then she looked down to the papers on her desk.

The sheriff shifted his gaze to Zack. "Did you identify yourself as a bounty hunter?"

No, he hadn't. "They didn't give either of us a chance to say anything before they assaulted us."

"They wouldn't *attack*, as you say, unless they felt threatened." Timmins fiddled with his handcuffs. "I should take you into custody."

"Sheriff, aren't you out of your jurisdiction?" Jessa remained on the couch. "We're in Gilliam, which is in Stenness County. Where are you from again?"

Zack grinned.

"Listen, little lady," Timmins began.

"Ouch," said one of his brothers.

"Uh-oh," said the other.

"Dumb," Lily whispered.

Like a rabbit on Easter Sunday, Jessa jumped off the couch and closed the distance between her and the lawman. "Excuse you? My name is Ms. Ross."

Timmins sneered. "I don't care if you're the Queen of England. If you interfere with my job, I'll haul you in, too."

Jessa's lips pressed together for a moment. "You know—" Before she could finish, Parker gripped her wrist, urging her to stay in place and shut up.

Their unwanted guest returned his gaze to Zack. "If you're not harboring Jamie, then you won't mind if I have a look around."

"Go ahead." Kyle waved the man through the office.

Timmins sauntered through the room and disappeared into the break room. His feet tapped the floor in an uneven rhythm. Kyle shot Zack another vicious glance. Zack pretended not to notice. The sheriff picked up his pace as he exited one room, passed behind Lily and entered the other room. When he came out, Kyle asked, "Are you done?"

"Almost." Timmins held up one finger. He turned and walked to the bathroom and closet. After another minute and some clattering of items on the closet floor, he returned to the front room. "Just so you know—" he strolled over to stand in front of Zack "—I will find her and you will pay for your crime."

Zack's nerves prickled. "Is that a threat?"

"No, it's a promise."

Still sounded like a threat to Zack.

Behind their unwanted company, Jessa shoved the front door open. "We'll be sure to let you know if and when we see the woman. Have a good day, Sheriff."

As Timmins passed by her, his gaze rolled over Jessa. Part of Zack waited for her to belt the guy. Part of him wished she would.

Once Jessa yanked the door closed behind Timmins, Zack's siblings began to talk at once and none of them to him. Not a problem. His brain focused on one thing: Timmins sliding into his front seat and driving away.

"Zack." Kyle's harsh voice sliced into his thoughts.

He turned around. "Huh?"

"Did you hear me? *I* am going to drop your woman off at the state police station."

"She's not *my* woman." He crossed the room and grabbed his truck keys.

As though Zack said nothing, Kyle continued, "You are staying here with Parker, Jessa and Lily."

"No." He clenched his keys in his palm.

Kyle narrowed his gaze. "What do you mean, no?"

Parker shook his head. "Little brother—"

"Stop treating him like a kid, Parker. He's not seventeen anymore. Zack, you need to take responsibility and make the right choice here. Think of your career."

The angst roiled tighter through him. Yes, the right choice. He straightened. "I won't let you take her in."

Kyle had forced him to put his career first all those years ago, but the circumstances were different this time. Zack had no emotional connection to Jamie. He just wanted to see justice upheld.

Like when they were kids, Kyle stood shaking his head and opening and closing his fists. But they were no longer children. They had a duty to help put criminals away and protect the innocent.

Jamie.

"I appreciate what you're trying to do and I respect your reasons," Zack explained, "but I cannot, in good conscience, turn her over. Not yet."

Kyle pointed to the back door. "Then you need to go."

"What?" Parker, Jessa and Lily said at once.

Their older brother kept his gaze on Zack. "If he won't follow the law, then he can't stay here."

Lily gasped.

"Wow," Jessa whispered.

"Kyle, think for a minute." Parker stepped between Zack and Kyle, as though to play referee.

"No. He either fixes this by turning her in or he runs with her before we take them both in."

Tension filled the room. Was Kyle really leaving him hanging out to dry? Knowing how much Zack valued his guidance, his brother stood here giving him an ultimatum? Kyle didn't get it. Jamie needed someone. Temporarily it would have to be Zack. He hoped he'd be good enough.

"Fine. We'll go." He pushed between his brothers and walked down the hallway.

"Zack, wait!" Parker called out even as Kyle kept arguing with him.

Zack shoved open the metal door.

\* \* \*

Heat surrounded Jamie, stifling her breathing. Something metal slammed against…maybe the building. Jamie froze. What if it wasn't Zack? The tailgate to Zack's truck opened seconds before the blankets and surfboard she'd covered herself with disappeared. Sunlight blinded her, but she couldn't miss the handsome man standing before her. Although at the moment, his jaw was tight and tension bunched his shoulders. "He's gone."

She rolled onto her knees and peeked around him. "Who?" Parts of her hair floated over her head as she met his gaze.

"Your brother-in-law came for you." As she climbed out of the truck, he reached forward to steady her with gentle hands. "I told him I turned you in to the Stenness County sheriff." Once he flipped the tailgate closed, he dangled the keys. "Go ahead and get in the front."

As Zack slid into the driver's seat, Jamie scooted into the passenger seat and set her backpack between her feet. With both hands, she smoothed out her hair. "What now?"

He stuffed the key into the ignition, then wrapped his hands around the steering wheel. "We move on, figure out our next step."

"Is your family going to help us?" Her stomach knotted, but she had to ask.

"No, we're on our own."

"I'm sorry."

He held up his hand. "Don't."

The word *sorry* itched to leave her lips again, but his narrow, accusing eyes stared her down. She lowered her head and threaded her fingers together. The knots in her belly tightened even more.

He blew out a breath. "I chose to help you," he said with softness in his voice. "They didn't."

"But still, it would've been great to have more people on our side."

"We have justice on our side. And God." He covered her hands with his own. "It'll work out."

A spark of hope flashed through her and she held on to his fingers for fear of losing confidence. Zack, she believed in. God? Not so much, not since He'd abandoned her after Erin died.

From the building came his sister. "Look." Jamie pointed.

As he turned his head, Zack lowered the window. "What's up? Did Kyle have a change of heart?"

The woman smirked. "No, listen. The sheriff will be looking for you any way he can. It'll be easy enough for him to tail you in your truck, but he won't be looking for my Jeep." She shoved her keys into his palm. "It's not a perfect plan, but it'll buy you some time."

"Are you sure you want to get involved, Lil?" He pulled his own keys free and handed them to her.

She nodded, clasped the windowsill and glanced at Jamie. "No woman or child should have to live in fear. I'll keep you in my prayers."

Jamie's voice cracked. Those were words she could've said to Erin if Jamie had kept her phone handy during the last morning of vacation. If she hadn't been so selfish. "Thank you."

Zack turned back to his sister and kissed her cheek. "What would I do without you?"

She smiled. "This is what big sisters are for. Now get going."

Once they'd switched vehicles, Zack shoved the key in

the ignition but didn't start the Jeep. "Jamie, I'm taking a lot of risks for you. I need you to tell me what's going on."

He was right. She owed him that much. "I'm pretty sure my brother-in-law killed my sister or had her killed. I also think he's involved in drug trafficking throughout the community."

"Do you have any proof?"

She shook her head. "Nothing concrete, but my sister mentioned having something incriminating against Drew. Plus, I've overheard students discuss buying drugs and all rumors point to the Ponahochet County Sheriff's Office. I intend to investigate, find evidence and take it to the state police."

For several seconds, Zack did nothing. Oh, what she'd give to know what thoughts crowded his mind.

After starting the Jeep, Zack headed south on the busy downtown roads.

Jamie chose to remain silent. Yes, the man had given up so much for her, but still… She'd never forgive herself if he got into trouble, whether with Drew and his deputies or the law-abiding police, because of her. She had enough guilt crushing down on her shoulders already.

But the reality was she couldn't leave him. She needed all the help she could get. Proving Drew was an evil man would take more than her tired teacher brain. The most challenging thing she ran across each day was trying to motivate high school kids to get papers written. Never had she dealt with people who broke the law. Nor had she had a bull's-eye on her own back.

No matter what, she had to focus on Charlotte. Everything she did had to be for her niece.

She glanced at her watch. Twelve forty-five. Charlotte would be having her lunch snack now. Jamie's heart squeezed in her chest. Leaving the little girl had been one of the hardest things to do, but life on the run was difficult enough for her alone. Charlotte wouldn't have done well. Plus, her presence would've taken Jamie's concentration away from her work. Putting her brother-in-law behind bars for his involvement with drugs, and maybe for her sister's death, had to remain Jamie's number one priority. It was the only way to make it up to her sister. Although, she still struggled with how best to make it happen.

"Hey, you okay?" Zack's fingers drifted along her arm.

A shiver rushed through her skin. "Yep, just thinking of my niece."

"Speaking of her, where do you have her stashed?" He flipped the blinker on and glanced behind him.

She'd known Charlotte's whereabouts would come up in conversation with Zack sooner or later. Now that he'd asked, she wasn't sure she was ready for the discussion. "Somewhere safe."

"Maybe we could go there to regroup. My guess is your brother-in-law will step up his attempts to find you."

She kept her gaze straight ahead. "I'm not taking you where Charlotte is."

"Why not? She might even have some information that could help us."

She shook her head. "Forget it, Zack."

"But if—"

"No."

Silence crept through the Jeep. He stared out the front window. "You don't trust me. Of course not, even after all I've been doing for you. Paint the big red sucker sign on my forehead."

Jamie winced. "I'm learning to trust you with my life, but I have to keep her safe. If anything happens to her, I'll never be able to forgive myself." She'd already failed her sister. "I'm sorry."

"Good to know where I stand." He clenched his teeth and shook his head. He refused to look at her and his fingers remained tight around the steering wheel.

A few times, she opened her mouth to cut through the tension, but what could she say? As good of a man as he appeared to be, she couldn't give him what he wanted.

They rode through the busy streets of Gilliam, getting caught behind too many red lights. Neither of them spoke, but she could still feel the tension drifting off Zack. Knowing she was the cause added another layer of guilt to her heart. Didn't she already have enough?

Zack pulled into the parking lot of an apartment building and parked by the door.

"Where are we?" she asked.

"My place, but only for a few minutes." He scanned the surroundings before turning the vehicle off. "We need to get out of here as soon as possible."

Jamie followed him to the front door. "Do you think Drew or George will come here?"

"Absolutely." He held the door open for her, then climbed the stairs in front of them. "It's the first place I'd check. As bounty hunters, we visit anyone and any place remotely related to the fugitive."

"But you're not wanted."

"To your brother-in-law I am."

Jamie followed him into the farthest apartment on the second floor and closed the door. Zack tossed his sister's keys onto his kitchen table. "Use the restroom down the hall if you need to but make it quick." Without another word, he disappeared into one of the other rooms.

Jamie stayed put in the center of the living room studying Zack's home. Rich, dark colors covered the mismatched furniture. A bookcase stood under the double window. On one shelf, he'd tucked away books about sports figures. On the lower shelf, a variety of classic tales stood next to faith-based books. Above the couch hung a picture of the Owen family. In it, Zack couldn't have been more than fourteen. Jamie smiled. If they'd gone to school together, she definitely would've had a crush on him. Even now she sometimes found it difficult to resist his charm.

But she had to. No sense mistaking his kindness for the offer of genuine friendship. Or something more. Ultimately, they'd go their separate ways.

The thought brought pressure around her heart.

A bland white valance above the kitchen window matched the generic table and appliances. Jamie leaned her hip against the kitchen sink. Three other cars sat in the parking lot outside.

When Zack returned to the kitchen, he tossed various items onto the table and began to shove them into a duffel bag. A first-aid kit, a small laptop along with its cords, a wad of cash, a leather packet with what looked like lock-picking tools, a bulletproof vest and a few other items she couldn't identify.

"Is all that necessary?" She hated how weak her voice sounded.

When he glanced over at her, his features softened to the way they were before she'd argued with him about where she'd hidden Charlotte. Once he picked up his duffel bag, he shifted around the chairs to stand beside her.

"Despite our differences, I still want to protect you." He raised his hand and brushed his thumb along her cheek. "And I'll do whatever is necessary to keep you safe."

She reached up for his arm. "Why?"

"Because you are worth it." When he looked at her like he was right now, she thought for sure he could see straight into her soul. That scared her on a whole different level, one she wasn't ready to examine.

She shifted her gaze to his mouth. Bad idea. His lips parted, tempted her. What would they feel like on hers? Would their first kiss be gentle, feather-like? Or would his mouth be more demanding, asking for something she wasn't sure she could give?

He leaned forward. Jamie closed her eyes as butterflies whirled to life within her. His male scent surrounded her. She waited for his kiss…

"We've got to go. Your brother-in-law's here."

"What?" Her eyes flew wide as she turned to glance out the window. In the parking lot, sprawled over two parking spaces, was a Ponahochet County sheriff's car.

# FOUR

Jamie swallowed the knot in her throat as she watched both Drew and George exit the vehicle…with guns drawn.

"Move." Zack pushed her toward the apartment door. "We'll go out the back of the building." After he picked up his sister's Jeep keys, he added, "Hurry."

Every nerve shook inside her. Could they get out in time?

Outside Zack's door, he grabbed her hand and tugged her behind him. They ran down the hallway in the opposite direction from the front entrance of his apartment building and rumbled down the carpeted stairs. A slamming sound filled the air. In her head, she pictured Drew kicking in the apartment door. Yelling voices filled the hallways.

She rushed to keep up with Zack. *Please don't let me fall.* Zack's hold tightened as he shoved the back door open and pulled her toward the side of the building. He picked up his speed. Jamie stumbled over the fresh flower bed.

When they reached Lily's vehicle, Jamie slid into the passenger seat and stared at the apartment building's front door. Would they get away before Drew and George realized their mistake? Beside her, Zack started the Jeep and shifted to Reverse. He took his time getting them across the parking lot. "Hurry, Zack."

"If I rush out, they'll know it's us. Right now, they're still in the building and probably tossing my apartment for clues about where I might take you."

Neither of them said anything for several minutes. As they joined the traffic, Zack kept glancing into the rearview mirror. Jamie twisted to stare out the back window. No cars rushed toward them and no blue-and-red lights flashed.

When she turned back around, she released a breath and stroked the cross necklace Erin had given her on her sixteenth birthday. To look at her, one might think she was calling on God, but Jamie had no illusions He would come to her aid. He'd given up on her, for sure. Maybe touching her favorite piece of jewelry, though, would give Jamie the courage she kept losing.

After another glimpse in the rearview mirror, Zack looked in her direction. "That was too close."

"Yeah." Both Drew's approach and the kiss. Her heart still worked too hard, but at least its pace had started to slow. How could she be thinking about kissing Zack while there was a price on her head? She was not important right now. She had a job to do: bring down her brother-in-law. Jamie had no right exploring romance.

They remained quiet for at least a good ten minutes. Zack swerved into a Dave's Marketplace parking lot, set the Jeep in Park and whipped out his phone.

"Who are you calling?" she asked as he dialed.

"Jessa, the woman who works with my brothers and me." He pressed the phone to his ear.

"I thought they wouldn't help us."

"I'm thinking she might be willing to, especially after

I tell her what happened and she does a little investigation." The woman must've answered because he shifted his focus away from Jamie. "Jessa…Yeah, we're still together. Listen, I need you to do something for me and I need you to keep it to yourself…Jamie's brother-in-law just raided my apartment. Can you keep tabs on it? Maybe swing by to see if he or the state police are investigating? If anyone asks, tell them I decided to stay with a friend out of town while I recover from my knee injury…No, I'll call you back…Yeah, you're right. You call me when you've got anything…Thanks."

Zack ended the call and dropped his phone in the console. The sound of it hitting the plastic sliced into the tension within the vehicle. Outside, traffic passed by like every other day. Would Jamie's life ever be normal again?

"Jamie, where's your niece?"

She shook her head. "No."

"I need to speak with her. She might have information about her parents you don't know about."

"You don't have anywhere else safe you could take us?"

"I don't usually get into trouble. Not anymore…not too much. At least none where I need to be sheltered." After shaking his head, he continued, "I'm a bounty hunter. Of course I can find us places to hide out, but we need to investigate your accusations." He shifted in his seat and draped his hand over the steering wheel. "I know you don't want to tell me, but being with your niece right now might be our best choice."

"I'm sorry. I can't." Charlotte was protected, tucked away out of state and living as carefree a life as Jamie and her friend Greta could give her. *I promise I'll keep her protected, Erin. For you.*

"You mean you won't." He stared at her with daggers

spitting from his eyes. She shifted in her seat. Where did the sensitive man from the apartment kitchen go?

"I appreciate all you've done to help me, but I won't give up my niece's location." Would he refuse to continue assisting her?

His jaw locked tight. For several more sickening seconds, he glared. She raised her chin and matched his gaze. She would not be bullied.

Zack yanked the door handle, escaped the vehicle and began pacing along the lines of the parking space.

Every moment Zack spent with Jamie Carter was more maddening than the last. He'd chosen to break her out of Timmins's jail with the intention of getting his family to find a way to help her. Going on the run with her had not been his plan. Every decision he made caused more confusion.

And thinking about kissing her? Unacceptable. He was not holding auditions for a new girlfriend. Romance had no business interfering with his job. If he intended to keep her safe, then he better get himself back on track. No attachments and definitely no kissing. Nope. None at all. Yes, he found her attractive and her devotion to her family matched his own, but there could never be anything between them.

"What now?" He leaned against the rear door and stared up to the sky. Was God trying to send him a message? If He was, Zack had no clue what the Father wanted from him. "I don't want to hurt her," he whispered.

But he'd been sure God wanted him to save Jamie from Timmins. He'd felt the tug on his humanity. Of course, he'd also expected God to guide him to a happy ending. Instead, crooked lawmen chased him, hired muscle shot at him and Jamie wouldn't cooperate. "I could use a little help here, a little guidance." Because the lines between his personal and professional worlds were blurring and honestly, he didn't like it one bit.

A young kid's laughter grabbed his attention. When he turned toward the grocery store, his inner angst unraveled. A mother smiled as she played with her child she'd placed in the store cart. Giggles lifted into the sky.

Jamie and her niece deserved the same freedom to be silly, carefree and safe. Whatever actions he decided on had to lead to justice. He had to trust in his faith and know God would be with him no matter what.

He glimpsed up at the sky again and smiled. "Thank You, Father."

With a lighter heart, he reentered the vehicle. "Okay."

"Is this where you tell me to get out because I'm too much trouble?" She grabbed the door handle. "That you don't want to be bothered anymore?"

*Wait, what?* "No. What I want is for you to work with me. Going on the run with you has tossed me into uncharted water. Frankly, I could use a little help."

"If you hadn't noticed, I'm not very good at this partner thing."

"Oh, yeah, I've noticed." Jamie may talk a good game, act tough and determined, but the wall around her heart wasn't as strong as she wanted the world to believe.

"I'm sorry," she whispered.

"Let's agree we'll both try harder to work together."

Tears sparkled in her eyes. "I still won't take you to Charlotte. I can't."

"I know." He'd leave the conversation about her niece alone. For now. He started the Jeep. "So, what's the first stop of our investigation?"

* * *

Jamie twisted her fingers in her lap. "I'd planned to go see my grandmother's best friend, Mrs. Cecily. Erin had mentioned her just before the phone went dead during her last call to my cell." According to someone else down Mrs. C.'s street, the old woman had been out of town since just before the school year ended. Jamie had been waiting since Erin's death to get in touch with her. Once Zack turned to her, she continued, "I have no idea what she can tell us, but I have to find out."

Zack pulled out of the parking lot and followed her directions to the woman's neighborhood. Thanks to late beach traffic, their progress was as slow as a turtle. She drummed her fingers on the edge of her seat.

After another fifteen thousand hours moving at a snail's pace, Zack pulled up outside Mrs. Cecily's house and turned off the ignition. He scanned the street. "Let's make this as quick as possible."

"I'll be back as soon as I can."

"You're not going without me."

She tried to stare him down like she did her obstinate high school students, but her skills had to be rusty. Zack refused to capitulate. "Fine, but let me do the talking." Once she'd stuffed her backpack under the seat, she slipped from the vehicle and closed the door.

Together they walked along the path to the front door. Bright summer sun warmed her back. Somewhere down the road, a lawn mower whirred as it trudged along. The scent of flowers brought back a flood of memories. She, Erin and their grandmother used to pick flowers and place them in each room of the house. Sometimes they'd share with Mrs. Cecily before she had her own garden.

Jamie's gaze fell on the metal cat statues by the front

steps. "Oh." She stopped and reached for Zack's arm. "You're not allergic to cats, are you?"

"No, why?"

They continued their walk. "I think at last count she had about fifteen."

His eyes widened. "Wow." A slow grin crossed his face, making him more attractive. With a wink, he leaned close enough for her to inhale the scent of him. "Don't worry, though. I'll protect you."

Butterflies tickled her insides. For a few precious moments, she was just Jamie Carter. No one was chasing her, no danger surrounded her and she actually smiled.

Zack pointed at her. "You should do that more often."

"What?"

"Smile. It brings out dimples I didn't even know you had and makes you even prettier."

Heat crept up her neck. "Thank you. You're not so bad yourself." Definitely not. With his attractive appearance and his good heart, she'd have a hard time finding a better man.

For some other woman. While enjoying a vacation, she'd let her sister down. Jamie had no right to be happy.

"Jamie, is that you?" The screen door squeaked as it opened.

Mrs. Cecily stood hunched over with age and a hard life. The woman had appeared to be a senior citizen when Jamie rode a bike with training wheels around the cul-de-sac. Now, she had to be nearing one hundred and fifty. She wore a casual muumuu and rust-colored slippers. Two cats stood as sentries and another slipped between Jamie and Zack.

"Yes, ma'am." She hugged Mrs. Cecily gingerly.

"So good to see you, dear!" She stepped back for them

to enter. Before either of them set foot inside the house, a series of meows welcomed them. Three more cats occupied the kitchen, two playing by the hallway and one sitting pensively by the back door. "And you brought your boyfriend, too." The older woman's gaze traveled down and up over Zack as she smoothed out her hair. "How wonderful."

"Uh, he's not… We're only…" Heat invaded Jamie's cheeks.

"We're friends. I'm Zack." He held his hand out to the older woman.

"Nice to meet you, Zack." Mrs. Cecily clutched his hand, then locked arms with him. "Please come in. It's so good to see one of these girls with a nice young man." As though Jamie wasn't even in the house, the lady led Zack through the hallway to the kitchen. "I was just making some coffee. Would you like some?" Faint meows announced the presence of more cats in other rooms.

"Uh, no, ma'am. We can't stay long. Thank you, though."

Mrs. Cecily stepped over one of the cats on her way to the counter. After opening a cabinet door, she grabbed more coffee cups. "I'll just get us some cookies, too." She opened another cabinet door and reached up for a bag of generic chocolate chip cookies. Her fingers stretched high but missed the bag.

"Here. Let me get it for you." Standing close to six feet tall, Zack easily reached the bag.

Another something Jamie couldn't peg stirred within her. The man was full of so many layers. Hard as nails when it came to keeping them safe and free, yet kind and careful with those who needed it. His lean frame still overtook the tiny kitchen. Or maybe it was his persona. Jamie had assessed him when he showed up at the internet café, but that had been quick with survival and escape in the center of her mind. Throughout today, she'd witnessed so much more tenderness than she ever thought possible from a man who'd first wanted to put her behind bars.

With strong hands, he assisted Mrs. Cecily to the kitchen table as gently as a newborn. What would it be like to have her hand latched on to his? How would it feel to have the physical support her body just noticed it missed?

No. She'd never have a husband. Her niece was all that mattered. Why waste her time considering the joys of a relationship, a partnership, she'd never be good enough to have? Doing so could only bring longing and loneliness.

"Jamie?" Zack waved his fingers in front of her.

"Huh?"

"Are you all right, dear?" Mrs. C. stroked the hair of yet another cat, this one on the kitchen table.

"Yes. I'm just tired. What did I miss?"

Zack sat across from the woman, trying hard to keep either of the cats at his feet from jumping on his lap. His hands gripped the coffee mug Mrs. C. shoved toward him. Jamie bit her lip to keep from laughing.

"Your boyfriend said you had some questions for me."

*He's not my boyfriend.* She released a heavy sigh. Should she even argue? "Right."

"Well, then, why don't you come join us?" Mrs. Cecily spoke to Jamie, but her gaze never left Zack. Leaning forward, she patted his forearm.

A grin tugged at the side of Jamie's mouth as she tiptoed around the pensive cat. She took the seat on the other side of Zack. "All right." She resisted the urge to cover his arm with her hand because none of her emotional yearning or romantic wishing mattered. She needed to focus on the reason for the visit.

The incessant noise of at least one cat meowing every minute hurt Zack's brain. He loved animals, even had a bunch growing up, but how could anyone live with this many?

"Jamie, I'm so sorry about your sister. My friend Nora, who picked me up from the airport, told me about her death."

Jamie nodded once. "Thank you. It's been difficult, but I'm getting through it day by day."

"I imagine your young man is helping you, as well."

Zack had no desire to be anyone's *young man*. His job was more important than any romantic relationship. The gas station attendant's injury all those years ago because of his emotional attachment to his girlfriend had spoiled that future for him. But if he had to be tied to another woman, Jamie might be a good choice.

Except, he didn't really know her.

"Yes, he is." Jamie stroked the side of her coffee mug. "Mrs. C., before my sister died, she mentioned your name on a message she left on my phone."

"Did she?"

"Yeah, but I didn't get the chance to talk to her."

With a wide, toothy smile, the old woman turned to him. "Oh, Jamie and Erin were so cute. I have lots of pictures of the family I could show you." Mrs. Cecily shoved her seat back, rested her palms on the table and pushed herself to standing.

Alarm flashed across Jamie's face. "Not necessary, Mrs. Cecily. He wouldn't be interested in those."

Zack chuckled. "Are you kidding? I'd love it." Jamie gripped his arm, pressed her lips together and gave him a death stare. "But we'll have to take a rain check, ma'am." Zack pried her fingers from his forearm, then covered the older woman's hand with his own. "Maybe some other time."

"Mrs. C., back to my sister." Jamie pushed a new cat away from her drink.

As she returned to her seat, Mrs. Cecily pressed her finger to her mouth and thought for a moment. "Yes, she visited a couple of days before I left for Maine. It was very odd since I hadn't seen her since her wedding. Mind, I loved seeing her and her precious little girl."

Zack took another sip of the worst coffee he'd had since his sister first learned to make it. "What sort of things did you talk about?"

"Oh, I can't remember all of it. She told me she was struggling in her marriage and how she would be making changes soon." The woman welcomed a second cat, the one harassing Jamie a few minutes ago, into her lap.

"What kind of changes?" Jamie asked.

"She didn't get specific. She only said she needed a better life for her and your niece. I didn't ask anything else because I didn't want to pry." She picked up her mug with both hands and sipped her coffee. "She also left me a key."

Zack caught Jamie's glance. He asked, "A key to what?"

"She didn't tell me. She just said since Jamie was out of town she needed someone else she could trust to hold on to it." She shrugged her shoulders. "I assume it's for her house. I suppose I can throw it away now."

"No!" he and Jamie said at the same time. If her sister

was as controlled by her husband as Jamie claimed, then passing the key on to someone else was a bold move for Erin. Trusting her old family friend with a key might've been to keep her and the kid safe.

Then again, it could be just a house key.

Mrs. Cecily moved her chair back again. "All right, then. I better get the key for you." Slowly she pushed herself to her feet. The cats in her lap thumped to the floor. Jamie held her hands together while her lips moved silently. Could she be praying?

The old woman shuffled her feet until she came to the key rack close to the back door. "Now, which one was it?" A jingling noise took the place of the old woman's voice as she sifted through everything hanging from the rack. "Got it!"

Zack gave up a silent prayer of his own. Jamie closed her eyes for a few seconds. When Mrs. Cecily returned to the table, she handed over the silver key. Jamie's hands went still as she read the key chain. Zack leaned over to see what it said. A hint of a flowery scent lingered in Jamie's hair.

*The key, Zack. Focus.* He read the plastic piece on the key ring. Brodigan Mail Kingdom. "Thank you, Mrs. Cecily."

"You're welcome, dear. Was I right? Is it for her house?"

Jamie clutched it close to her chest and looked up. "No, but I'm hoping it'll be for something much more important."

Could it be so easy? Would this tiny piece of metal hold the proof needed to uncover the crooked sheriff's devious ways with hurting his wife and feeding illegal drugs into his community? "Thank you for the coffee,

Mrs. Cecily, but we really need to get going." He stood, then Jamie followed.

"It was lovely to meet you, Zack, and wonderful to see you, Jamie. Again, I'm sorry about your sister's passing. Please know I'm keeping you and your niece in my prayers."

"Thank you." The two women embraced.

Zack held out his hand to urge Jamie down the hall.

She started toward the front door. Zack followed, with the shuffling feet of the older woman behind him. "Be sure to stop by when you have more time. I'd love to show you those pictures."

"Thank you, ma'am." Zack held the door open for Jamie. "I'll definitely be back." He had to admit, checking out Jamie as a kid intrigued him. Was she a girlie girl, always in dresses with her hair done fancy, or did she prefer jeans, T-shirts and ponytails like she wore today? Either way she was pretty. Her determination, the way her face lit up when she smiled, her courage fighting her own Goliath—all of these things made her even more attractive.

For another man. Zack had no desire to get caught up in a woman again. No, thank you. His career was more important.

When they'd stepped onto the walkway, Jamie glanced back to him. "She's nice enough, but she can be overbearing at times. And nosy. And she was always disappointed with me for not following her faith."

"We all have to follow our own path."

She snorted. "I'd have to have faith first."

Zack's heart squeezed. How sad to go through life not knowing the Father. Zack had been fortunate enough to grow up in a family with a solid faith. "Maybe you need to recharge your God batteries."

"I think one dropped out when He let a drunk driver take my parents. The other fell out when my sister got involved with Drew."

"I'm sorry about your family tragedies, but remember you're always welcome in His world."

She pulled the passenger-side door open. A soft breeze lifted loose strands of her hair across her lips. "I wish I had your faith." Such sadness came in her words.

"You can."

She glanced toward the center of the cul-de-sac. "It would take too long for me to find the road back to Him, let alone walk it."

Zack pulled his own door open. "Then follow me."

She smiled and returned her gaze to him. "You make it sound so easy."

"Oh, no. Definitely not. There are a lot of potholes along the path, but if you look where you're going and trust in Him, you'll recognize the help God's giving you and all He has to offer."

"Well, one step at a time." She rubbed the back of her neck. The cries of a child sailed through a window screen. In the distance, a young boy called out to a barking dog.

"We should get going. Even though Mrs. C. isn't directly related to you, Timmins could still find the connection."

Once they slid into the Jeep and closed the doors, Zack placed one hand on the steering wheel and turned the key in the ignition. Hopefully whatever was in the lockbox would be enough to support the theory that the good sheriff was not so good.

Jamie clapped her hands together. "All right. Let's head to Brodigan Mail Kingdom. I need to know what's in the box."

*I need.* She said the same words a lot.

Once he started driving down the street, he asked, "Why a mail center, though? Why not a safe-deposit box in a bank?"

She shrugged. "Maybe Erin was too worried the bank staff would contact Drew. Or maybe she didn't feel confident enough to open a safety box in another bank outside of Hampton, where she and Drew lived." Sadness locked some memory in her thoughts.

As he stopped at a stop sign, he gave her a weak smile. "We'll figure it out."

"I'm so grateful to you for putting your life on hold to help me."

"Forget it," he said.

"No, I won't." A sheen of moisture covered her eyes, making them sparkle. "You're a good man, Zack. Most people would have left me in Drew's jail cell. No matter what happens, I will always be thankful for your presence in my life."

Part of him wanted to soothe her worries. No matter what crimes she'd committed, she deserved to be safe. When she looked at him like that, like her hope fell to him, another part of him wanted to run the other way. Yes, he was assisting her right now, but he'd hand the job over to anyone if he could. Too fast he was growing connected to her. No, Zack definitely didn't like the position he'd put himself in.

The car behind them honked its horn. Right. The mailbox. Zack continued driving through the intersection. "Is there an address on the key chain?"

"Twenty-nine Chester Avenue."

Hopefully they'd find enough evidence to put her brother-in-law away. Then she could take her and her niece's future back into her own hands and he could get back to training for his next surfing competition.

The ride took close to a half hour. With each passing mile, Jamie's nerves tightened a bit more. When she inched forward until the seat belt stopped her, she tapped her fingers on the dash. Out of the corner of her eye, she could see Zack glancing her way. She captured her fingers in her other hand. "Sorry."

He shook his head. "Not a problem."

"Turn left." She pointed. Almost there. If Erin felt she had to hide the information, then it had to be incriminating, right? "Over there."

Zack pulled into the parking lot of a shopping plaza, slid in between two pickups, then turned off the vehicle. "It doesn't happen to have a box number on it, does it?"

She studied the key chain. Once she brushed off dust, she found three black numbers ridged into the metal. "One-thirty-three."

"All right." Zack opened his door. "Let's go and let's make it fast."

Together they made their way into the business. Cool air breezed through her hair and along her neck as they stepped inside. Soft music played in the background, not elevator music but almost as bad. A middle-aged woman stood behind the counter taping up a box the size of a toaster. She glanced their way but said nothing. Before they moved on, the woman peered at the silent TV in the corner behind her, then back to them. An old man wrapped in a sweater stood at the counter near the far wall writing something with a shaky hand.

"This way." Zack caught hold of her elbow and guided her toward the walls of silver mailboxes. Big fat ones, rectangular thin ones. She gripped the key in her hand as they both studied the numbers on the boxes. Up one aisle, down the next.

A commercial on the radio station burst through the speaker. Jamie gasped and planted her palm on her chest. Zack whirled around. When his gaze fell on her, tenderness sneaked through. He placed his palms on her shoulders. Warmth seeped through the fabric of her shirt and soothed her frayed nerves. "We're okay."

She nodded. "I know." *For now.*

"We're going to find this box, grab whatever's inside, then we'll be on our way. Easy, right?" After a squeeze, he released her and resumed the hunt for her sister's mailbox.

She crossed the aisle and searched. "Here." She pointed to a thin box not much bigger than an average-sized hardback book.

Zack hovered behind her, close enough for her to breathe in his scent.

She slid the key into the lock. With ease, she turned it to the left, then opened the door. "Bingo!" Inside was a bulky envelope. A shade of relief flowed through her. Maybe the whole ordeal could soon be over, Charlotte could come home and Drew would be sent behind bars for breaking the laws he'd sworn to uphold.

Maybe then the shards of guilt would stop clawing at her. Then she could properly take over her role as a pseudo-mom.

Zack reached into the box and grabbed the item. As

he studied the envelope, Jamie closed and locked the mailbox. "Does it say anything?"

"Nothing on the outside. We'll worry about what's inside once we're out of here." With her by his side, he headed toward the door.

"Uh, wait." The clerk ran out from behind the counter. "Are you going to pay the bill for the box?"

"Not today." Zack stepped around her, ready to maneuver through the exit.

The woman moved back, blocked their exit. "But I need the money for the…" She glanced around them toward the connected stores. "For the…"

Jamie and Zack followed her gaze around. Two men with uniforms and weapons rushed toward them from the attached mall.

Uh-oh.

# FIVE

God forgive Zack for using an intimidation tactic with an innocent woman. "Look, I don't want to hurt you so you need to move out of our way." He flinched inside.

The clerk darted to his left. Zack and Jamie rushed out of the mail center.

"Hey, she's wanted!" the clerk hollered.

Jamie turned back to the building. "How does she know who I am?"

"She must've seen your picture somewhere." Out of the corner of his eye, Zack caught sight of the uniformed men approaching the door of the mail center.

"My picture? What about yours?"

"You're the fugitive."

Right. Her case. His job. Somewhere along the line he'd shifted further into caring for the victim.

Woman.

Criminal.

"Stop right there!" One mall cop stayed with the clerk and spoke into his radio. The other, the tougher looking one, followed Jamie and him outside, closing the distance between them at an alarming rate. "We said wait." The guy grabbed Jamie's injured arm.

"Ow!" She doubled over.

Zack's gut clenched with her cry. "Let her go." He

slammed a jab into the other man's jaw, then another punch to his stomach. While the man stumbled back a few steps, Zack grabbed Jamie's hand. "Come on!" The other guard charged through the doorway.

Zack and Jamie ran farther into the parking lot, opened the doors and slid inside his sister's vehicle. Somewhere in the distance, a siren began to wail.

Great. Nothing like drawing attention to yourself when you're trying to be invisible. He dropped Erin's envelope into Jamie's lap. As Zack shoved the gear into Reverse, Jamie stared out her window. "We're already in the Jeep. Why would these guys still be running after us?"

"Probably trying to catch the license plate." As he pounded his foot on the gas, he shook his head. "I never should have switched vehicles with Lil. What was I thinking?" He wasn't. He was too caught up in…Jamie.

Once they slid into the traffic, a police car drove into the parking lot. Zack needed to get rid of Lil's Jeep but he also needed another vehicle. And fast. Once they'd crossed into Gilliam, Zack pulled into a grocery store parking lot. Picking up his phone, he analyzed their situation. He needed a car, but he refused to steal a vehicle. Unless he absolutely had to. He punched in the numbers and waited for his sister to pick up.

"Z, I was wondering when you'd call."

"Anyone in the office?" He didn't want to get her in trouble with their brothers.

"No, they're out on a run. What's up?"

"I need a new vehicle."

"You didn't total my Jeep, did you?" Her voice held half worry and half annoyance. The reference to when he crashed her old Mustang made him wince.

"No, I'm a better driver than when I was fourteen.

Listen, Jamie's pulled me into a disaster and it's going to get worse before it gets better. It's bad enough I'm involved. I don't want to drag you down with us, too. And trust me, the crooked sheriff will come after you if he thinks it will benefit him."

Jamie turned to him with the look of a wounded puppy. Blood stained her shirtsleeve again from where the guard had grabbed her. Zack's conscience gnawed at him. He'd said some harsh words about her in his conversation with Lil.

"Okay, let me think," Lily said. Seconds ticked by. "I have a neighbor who's out of town for the summer. I'm watching her place."

"Would she be okay with us borrowing her car?" Beside him, Jamie struggled to open her sister's envelope.

"As long as you don't destroy it. How about I meet you in the mall parking lot by the food court with my friend's car and we'll switch?"

"Sounds like a plan." He ended the call and turned to Jamie. She ripped one corner of the well-taped envelope.

"Let me help." He reached forward.

She pulled away and slid one finger inside the package. "I've got it."

With a tender voice, he said, "Jamie, about my comments to Lily about your…situation…" She expected him to be professional, to stay on her side and he'd decided to let frustration overtake him. "I had no right to be a jerk. I was just—"

"Forget it."

So, she wouldn't allow him to apologize. Stubborn woman.

Determined.

Not afraid to speak her mind. She accepted some help

with the dangerous aspect of her situation, but he had no doubt she'd still be strong on her own, too.

Stop. He had to stay focused on his job, not his feelings about the woman. He had to focus on what really mattered: gathering enough information to help prove Jamie was justified in stealing her niece and going after her brother-in-law.

Jamie turned her sister's envelope upside down and dumped the contents in her lap. A journal, a couple pieces of paper written in Erin's handwriting, a set of pictures of Drew and some sleazy-looking men.

Zack studied the cover of the journal, probably reading the Bible verse on it. "Is this your sister's?"

After skimming the first entry, dated March 18, she shook her head. "Nope. It's not Erin's handwriting." Beth McKutchen's name was on the inside cover. Several pages were written on, but the majority of the journal was blank. "This belonged to Beth, Drew and Erin's housekeeper until just before—" *I left my sister to fend for herself*"—Drew killed Erin."

"She quit?" Zack shifted in his seat and glanced down at Beth's book.

Jamie shrugged. "Or Drew fired her, which is more likely."

"Why?"

"If Beth started asking too many questions or maybe started to get close to my sister, Drew wouldn't have liked it. He'd do whatever he needed to keep Erin under his control." She continued to skim the pages. "Why would Beth's diary be in my sister's mailbox?"

"Here's a list of names." Zack picked a slip of paper off Jamie's knee. The touch of his fingers sent a shiver

through her. "Do you know any of them?" His close prox-
imity tugged away her concentration.

She shook her head. Her number one priority was to
study the notes in her lap. "Some sound familiar, but I
couldn't tell you where I'd heard them before."

Zack unfolded another piece of paper. "This has a
Hampton Waterfront address." He picked up the photos
and began showing them to her. "What about these pictures?"

"I don't recognize anyone in them except Drew and
George." She grabbed the one he'd just set down on the
console. "Oh, wait. That's Charlie, one of the deputies
who tried to grab me in the park."

After another glance at all the paperwork in her lap,
Jamie sat back and rubbed her eyes. "This opens so many
more doors yet I still feel lost." She'd thought the visit to
Brodigan Mail Kingdom would solve the problems Jamie
had created for herself by grabbing her niece. Instead,
for the moment, they made the quest for the truth harder.

"Don't get discouraged. I usually have less information than this on a fugitive and I still find them. We've
got Beth's journal, which might give us something, a
list of men's names, pictures of your brother-in-law with
various guys and an address down by the waterfront.
Now we need to be smart and plan the next steps in our
investigation."

Jamie stuffed the items into her backpack. "But first,
we need to meet your sister."

"Right." Zack headed toward his and Lily's meeting
spot. His sister sat waiting when he pulled up outside the
food court entrance. Five minutes later, they'd switched
Lily's Jeep with a sedan and Jamie and Zack watched
his sister drive away in her own vehicle.

"Now, let's get your arm patched up before we head out again." He twisted in his seat and grabbed something out of his duffel bag. As Jamie glanced at her bloodied shirt, Zack opened the first-aid kit on his lap.

Once she'd lifted her sleeve, he got to work cleaning the wound. Again. Zack's hands remained gentle despite the occasional twinge of discomfort in her skin. She closed her eyes and paid attention to the rhythm of her heartbeat.

"Am I hurting you?"

"No. I'm trying to relax."

"Are you scared?"

"About my arm? No."

"How about the whole ordeal with Timmins?"

She hesitated, but why? Zack already knew more about her in the time they'd been together than most people learned over several months. How had that happened?

"Every day I wonder if I'm strong enough. Can I make Charlotte's life safe and happy? Will I be able to convince others how evil Drew is? I'm used to attempting to change people's minds, but it's a lot different working with teenagers than adults. Add that to my illegal activities... This is all new to me and, if I can be honest, pretty frightening." And she'd probably have to hunt down a new job after breaking so many laws.

They remained quiet as he finished up. Once he'd replaced the bandage, he covered the new one carefully with his palm, sending warmth throughout her. "You are strong enough. Have faith."

"In God?"

"Yes, but also in yourself. You're a smart woman."

Knots formed in her stomach. Should she keep her mouth shut? But the words wouldn't wait. "I know I wasn't what you bargained for when you got to work, but thank you for everything you've done and continue to do for me." She covered his hand with her own. "I'm not sure what path I should take, but you replaced the strength I started to lose in my battle with Drew."

His deep green eyes sparkled as a flash of surprise crossed his handsome face.

For a moment, Jamie allowed her thoughts to wander. What would it be like to have a man like Zack in her life? Someone to talk to, someone to back her up, someone to cherish her as much as she cherished him.

But she had no time for romance, no right to expect a long-lasting, intimate relationship. Her only duties had to be bringing Drew to justice and giving Charlotte a safe and happy life. To do that, she needed to be at the top of her game.

As proof that she wasn't, she wrestled with a yawn.

After a glimpse at her mouth, Zack tucked her free-flying strands of hair behind her ear. A shiver rippled down her spine. Was he aware of the effect his touch had on her? If he was, he kept it to himself. Unlike other points in the day, she couldn't read him at all.

"We should stop for the night." He shifted in the seat, started the engine and slid the car into evening traffic. "We'll stop to get something to eat then head to a motel my family and I have used before in tracking down fugitives. It's nothing special, but it is clean. We'll lay low and get some rest."

"Good thinking." She needed time away from him to bring her focus back where it belonged. "I'll read Beth's journal and see if she gives us any information. How about in the morning we go through the names on the list and look them up? Then we can head down to the address on the waterfront." Tomorrow was soon enough to continue their journey together.

"Sounds like a plan."

Jamie sat on the edge of the full-size bed and towel-dried her hair in front of the slightly cracked mirror. Sunshine fell through the windows and made a path across the carpet. Last night, here in a generic motel in downtown South Gilliam, had been her best sleep in ages. How did that happen? Knowing Zack was next door had surely helped. What would it be like to sleep soundly every night? Too often it had felt like she'd never get the chance again.

But this morning, excitement rippled through her. After reading the journal last night, she had so much to share with Zack. Yes, the diary was Beth's, but Erin had written in it, too.

The excitement, if she were honest with herself, was also due to Zack himself. Her thoughts kept drifting to the kiss they'd almost shared yesterday. As butterflies swirled through her belly, she smiled. Zack had been gentle with his touch so far. Chances were his kisses would be the same. Thoughts of them going on a date to the newest beachside restaurant surfaced in her mind. They could get to know each other more and she'd be able to focus on him, his charming smile, his handsome face and his strong faith. "Wishful thinking," she whispered to herself. Zack deserved better than her.

A soft knock interrupted her thoughts. She stilled, stared at her backpack where she'd set it under the table.

"Jamie, it's me," Zack's muffled voice called from the other side of the door.

"Hold on." Once she'd unlocked the two dead bolts

and chain, she opened the door to him. Heat and humidity pushed inside.

"Good morning." He smiled over several paper bags. The scent of bacon and eggs sailed toward her and her stomach growled.

"Hi." She stepped back and motioned him inside the room.

"I wasn't sure what you liked to eat so I picked up a bunch of items." He stood by the table and began pulling wrapped food out of the bags.

She grabbed a breakfast sandwich. "Anything is good. Thank you."

He sat across from her and pointed toward a bag he'd left on the floor. "I also picked up a change of clothes. I wasn't sure what might fit so I went with as generic as I could."

While he set out two coffees, she fished through the bag at her feet. A casual turquoise T-shirt and a hunter green one, along with a travel kit of personal items. "Thank you, Zack. Of course I'll pay you—" *when we're out of this mess* "—at some point." For now, she needed to keep whatever funds she still had. Using an ATM anywhere would help Drew track her.

Zack waved her off. "Don't worry about it."

If he kept being so nice to her, he might break down another part of the wall around her heart. She couldn't let that happen. Believing in fairy tales would only hurt her more in the end.

"Hey, I've got some news."

"What's up?" he asked.

"Beth started the journal when she began working at my sister's. It has the average diary stuff in it at first, but then she talks about being nervous around Drew.

She wrote notes about what she saw and heard and she used the journal to keep track of her thoughts and investigating."

Zack's eyes widened. "What investigating did she do?"

"Remember I told you there were rumors about drugs being sold to teens in Hampton and nearby towns?" He nodded as he took another bite of his sandwich. "Apparently her youngest sister, who's a junior, told her the rumors were true. So Beth began interviewing some of the kids at the high school for more information. Her last entry was her last day of work."

"Wow. It seems we're on the right path."

Jamie set her breakfast sandwich down and wiped her hands. "That's not all." She stood, grabbed the journal off the nightstand and handed it to him. "Erin wrote in there. It was more stream of consciousness, but she talks about how Beth had been helping her and how she wonders why Beth left her and Charlotte."

"Which reminds me. Why would Beth have the journal at the house if she had information about Timmins? That seems risky and reckless."

Jamie shrugged. "Maybe she got tired of working to help Erin and decided to leave it there and wash her hands of the whole thing."

Zack shrugged. "It's something to think about."

After another bite of her sandwich, she continued, "Erin also wrote Beth's address, with a note to visit as soon as she could. Her last entry mentioned how tense everything was in the house and how she intended to continue her and Beth's work so maybe she could finally get away from Drew. Maybe that's when she decided to open the account at Brodigan Mail Kingdom."

Silence took over as they both continued to eat. After a minute, Zack said, "Our first stop today needs to be Beth's address." He took a bite of a hash brown and swallowed. "After I left you last night, I did some research online. I wanted to see what the press thought of your sister's death, Timmins, you."

"I could've told you it's all bad. To the rest of the world, Drew is the good guy distraught over all that's happened, my sister's death was tragic and I'm crazy."

He opened his mouth to respond but must've changed his mind. Instead, he crumbled up one of his wrappers and tossed it toward the trash bin by the dresser. It landed on the floor. "Timmins says you assaulted him once you found out your sister was dead." Zack fished through a paper bag for another sandwich.

Jamie nodded while she swallowed a bit of a hash brown. "That part is true. I returned home from a vacation with some friends from school and drove straight over to see my sister—" *because Erin had begged for help* "—and saw the crime scene tape. By then, she'd been dead three hours and Drew's office hadn't bothered to contact me. There were neighbors all over the place, two other sheriff's department cars were parked in the driveway and a paramedic had Charlotte. I pulled my niece in my arms and held her until Drew tried to take her away. I kind of went crazy then and lashed out at him. I started blaming him and hollering to anyone who'd listen that he should be investigated because the circumstances surrounding Erin's death were a little too suspicious."

"Why'd he arrest you?"

Heat rose to her cheeks. This part of the story she was ashamed of. "I went after him. I grabbed an IV pole from the back of the ambulance, ran up to him and swung. He shoved me from the front and I had another man grabbing me from behind. I hit him, too, but he kept his hold on me. A female deputy grabbed the pole, then tried to check out Drew's injury, but he shoved her away, too. Next thing I know I've got cuffs on and I'm locked in the back seat of a sheriff's car."

"Your brother-in-law says he's worried about your niece's safety."

Rolling her eyes, she finished chewing. "He knows I'd never do anything to hurt her."

"He claims if you brought Charlotte back he'd be willing to drop the charges against you."

"I wouldn't believe anything he says." Jamie took a sip of coffee. "Did you call your partner, the one looking into Drew's invasion of your apartment?"

He nodded. "She got there and one of my neighbors told her the place had been tossed but the police were looking into it. The neighbor had seen the sheriff's car and probably assumed they were taking care of it. Jessa went into my apartment, but she couldn't tell if anything had been taken."

"But you don't live in Drew's jurisdiction. Wouldn't your neighbor question why the Ponahochet County sheriff would be investigating?"

"Most people don't understand how law enforcement works."

"True. Until my sister's death, I had no idea what it entailed."

"I also asked Jessa to look into drug use and arrests within the schools in and around Hampton. She'll get back to me when she's got something to report." Zack crumpled another set of wrappers. "What's the connection between Timmins and Deputy Linden?"

"They've been friends since middle school, both on the football and wrestling teams. They got into a lot of trouble together in high school, then got respectable jobs and supposedly became respectable men. They're still pretty close, like brothers." Jamie gathered her wrappers, rose and dropped the trash into the bin. "A couple of his other deputies are friends from school, too."

Zack crumpled the rest of the wrappers on the table and pitched them one by one toward the can across the room. Several bounced off the rim and landed at Jamie's feet. She smiled as she reached down for them. "Great shots."

Zack kept his gaze on her, a lazy grin of his own twisting his lips. "What can I say? Basketball was never my sport."

Once she threw out his trash, she moved toward the mirror and ran her fingers through her still-wet hair. "What sport did you play?"

"Football mostly, baseball when I got to high school. How about you? Did you play anything?"

Settling across from him once again, she folded her arms on the table and chuckled. "No, I was never coordinated enough."

He narrowed his gaze on her as though focusing. "Choir?"

As she smiled wider, she shook her head. "Can't hold a note."

"Band?"

"Nope."

After a few seconds, he pointed toward her. "Checkers."

"Sorry."

"So, what did you do for an extracurricular activity in high school?"

She clasped her fingers and tucked them under her chin to keep from covering her face.

"Come on, you know you want to tell me."

He was right. Talking to him was easier with each moment they spent together. "I was on the debate team and I was president of the math club."

His eyes crinkled at the corners as he burst into laughter.

"Stop laughing at me." She playfully slapped his forearm.

A comfortable silence settled into the room. Sharing the silly conversation made her feel normal, less afraid.

He took hold of her hand and rubbed his thumb along the back of it. With each swipe, a bit more ease took over her heart. "I'm glad you took my advice."

"Which was?"

"To smile more."

Remembering his compliment outside Mrs. C.'s house about how pretty she was made heat travel up her neck. *Zack can't be a romantic interest, remember?* How could she be allowed to have a happy ending when she'd failed her sister? She slid her hand free of his and instantly felt the loss of his touch. Foolish to allow herself to remember she was a woman first.

Jamie stood and swiped the table clean. "Let me change, then we can go." She grabbed one of the new shirts from under the table. "Hopefully Beth will be willing to help us and explain why she stopped investigating Drew."

\* \* \*

When Zack pulled into Beth McKutchen's street, Jamie's stomach roiled. Would the woman be willing to work with them in their investigation? Who was to say Beth would even want to listen to Zack and her?

As Jamie stuffed her backpack under the seat, Zack turned off the ignition. They exited the vehicle and approached the front door. Boys' whoops and hollers floated from somewhere close by. Her gaze scanned the dead-end road. Kids played a front yard game of football a few houses down.

She raised her hand and knocked. Several moments later, someone unlocked a dead bolt. The door slid open, but the screen door remained closed. Probably locked, too.

An older blonde woman stood before them with enough suspicion in her expression to force Jamie back a step. But Zack braced her, pressed his palm against her back.

"Can I help you?" The woman's words held the grittiness of a lifelong smoker and the bronze of her skin made it look like rubber. Jamie had only met Beth once, but she could see the McKutchen family resemblance in this woman's features. Beth's mother, maybe? Or much older sister?

"Hi, I'm Jamie Carter."

The woman nodded. "I know who you are. I saw you on the news with Sheriff Timmins." She crossed her arms. "What do you want?"

"We're sorry to bother you, ma'am, but we were hoping to speak with Beth. Does she live here?" Zack asked.

The woman's expression turned to stone. Her fingers tightened around her biceps. "Are you serious?"

"We won't take long," Jamie said.

"We have some questions for our investigation," Zack added, "and we're hoping she can help us connect the dots."

The woman's eyes narrowed. "Beth can't help you." She stepped to one side and grabbed the door handle.

Zack said, "Ma'am, we're sorry if we're upsetting you for some reason, but this is important. We need to talk to her."

"So do I, but my daughter's been missing for a month."

# SIX

"Missing? What do you mean?" Jamie's knees knocked. This had to be her brother-in-law's doing. From somewhere close by, birds mocked her with a pleasant tune.

"Gone, not here, no longer around." Beth's mom remained rooted to her spot, but at least she wasn't slamming the door in their faces.

"What happened?" Zack asked.

"We don't know. She left for work one day. Then she was gone."

"I'm sorry to hear it. Can we please come in? I have a feeling we'll be able to help each other." Hope drained out of Jamie with every silent second.

"Ma'am," Zack began, "I promise I will do whatever I can to help find your daughter."

Telling this woman any details was a risk, but the way Jamie saw it, she and Zack didn't have a choice. "We're trying to find evidence to prove my brother-in-law and Deputy Linden are criminals."

Mrs. McKutchen scoffed. "You're fighting an uphill battle, aren't you?"

The woman didn't know the half of it. "Your daughter was brave enough to assist my sister. Please, let's work together."

The older woman narrowed her gaze at them for a

solid five seconds. Finally, she stepped back and opened the door wide. "I suppose it can't hurt."

Zack held the screen door as Jamie stepped inside. The stench of stale smoke assaulted her as she followed the woman farther into the living room. Several pictures covered the walls, mostly of the missing woman. The lady shoved a few newspapers to one side of the couch. "Have a seat."

Jamie and Zack squeezed together on the empty part of the couch. Their thighs touched, which was oddly comforting.

A cushion whooshed as their hostess plopped into the nearby rocking chair. "Now, what questions do you have?" On the coffee table sat a pack of cigarettes, a bowl of individually wrapped candies, a coffee mug still steaming and a handful of papers.

"When did your daughter go missing?" Zack asked.

"Just over a month ago. She left the house at the regular time for work, took the car and no one heard from her again. Sheriff Timmins called her cell phone and then her boyfriend to find her when she didn't show up for work."

"What about the car?" Out of the corner of her eye, Jamie caught a puppy sleeping below the window.

"They found it abandoned under a bridge along the highway. It had smashed into the cement wall and the only fingerprints were Beth's. They supposedly found drugs hidden in the glove compartment."

"What do you mean *supposedly*?" Zack leaned forward and dropped his forearms to his thighs. His elbow settled on her knee.

"My daughter never did drugs. She had medical issues, but even without those she had too much respect for herself to use drugs." She grabbed a candy out of the pewter bowl, yanked off the wrapper and shoved the piece into her mouth.

Jamie inched forward, folded the candy wrapper and left it on the table. "What happened to the investigation into Beth's disappearance?"

"It stalled. The detectives looked hard at her boyfriend, but he had an alibi for the time frame of her disappearance. They questioned me, the rest of our family, plus her friends, and got nothing. After a while, the police stopped looking, as if they didn't think her life meant anything because they claimed she did drugs." The woman stared across the room and grabbed a few of the chocolates from the table. Her hand shook slightly. "I had a gut feeling, you know?" Tears shimmered in her eyes but didn't fall.

"About what?" Zack entwined his fingers. He'd sat the same way a few times since Jamie had met him, revealing his concern, his care for people and the truth, the gentleness...

She closed her eyes. Zack was only temporary. Focus on Beth, the woman who'd gone missing, most likely because she helped with the fight to get Erin free.

"Your brother-in-law was always an overbearing individual. Of course, I'd only seen him a couple of times, but he never really looked at me. I often trust my gut feeling about people when I first meet them and I had a bad feeling about him from the start of Beth's job."

Zack turned to Jamie. "How long had she worked for your sister?"

"Three, four months." Jamie shifted in her seat.

Mrs. McKutchen popped another candy in her mouth at the same time her gaze traveled to the pack of cigarettes at the other end of the table. "Sheriff Timmins didn't like my daughter or how close she got to your sister."

How close she'd gotten since Jamie was too busy. Another punch in the stomach.

Beth's mother grabbed her cup of coffee and took a sip. "Now it's your turn. What can you tell me?"

Jamie began, "She'd over—"

Zack squeezed her thigh. "Not much. We're still investigating the connection between your daughter and Drew Timmins. Let me ask you one more question. Do you know the name of the officer who first investigated Beth's disappearance?"

"Sheriff Timmins had Deputy Linden run the investigation since he wasn't involved with Beth socially or professionally." She leaned over to switch out the coffee mug for the pack of cigs. "You're not going to share any of your information with me, are you?"

Zack pulled his keys from his pocket. "We have a lot of puzzle pieces we're still having trouble connecting."

What? How cruel could he be to a grieving mom? No, Jamie wouldn't go against Zack's wishes right now, but he wouldn't stop her from attempting to ease the woman's pain later. Jamie grabbed Mrs. McKutchen's empty hand. "I promise you I'll come back when we have more information."

"Then maybe I'll know what happened to my baby girl." Tears touched the older woman's cheeks. She lowered the cigarette pack, then covered Jamie's fingers. "I don't have any reason to, but I believe you. The good Lord is telling me to trust you."

Jamie slowly pulled her hands away. There He went again: guiding others yet leaving her to fight for every scrap of information she could get to free her niece and herself. It was as though He wanted to punish her for letting her sister down. And letting Him down.

"Thank you for your time, ma'am." As he stood, Zack cupped Jamie's elbow and urged her to follow his lead.

Beth's mom walked them to the door. "Thank you for giving me hope that I might get some kind of closure."

*Closure*. A loaded word with the potential to crush someone's heart or lift it up. Unfortunately, Jamie had little hope Beth would be found alive.

Once she and Zack drove out of the neighborhood, she rubbed her temple. "You know what I'm thinking?" Darkening clouds pushed the sunlight around.

"Besides the very real possibility Timmins had something to do with Beth's disappearance?"

"Yeah, I mean he may've stepped back from the investigation officially, but having George run it wasn't much better." She shook her head. "Maybe Beth left her journal with Erin because she knew Drew was onto her and she didn't have time to contact the police."

"Could be."

"I wonder if Beth going missing was the catalyst for my sister wanting to get out of the marriage."

Zack eased the car into the traffic on the highway. "What if Timmins and Linden were worried about how much Beth knew about whatever they're involved in? What if they got rid of her, staged the car wreck and planted the drugs to discredit her?"

"I'd say it worked." She brushed some flyaway strands of hair behind her ear. "We'll find a way to prove it. I have to have faith." Maybe God would forgive her at some point.

Zack grinned. "You? Faith?"

"What can I say?" She shrugged. "We've been together long enough you're starting to influence me."

He nodded once. "That's God working through me."

She'd meant for her words to lighten the mood, but awkwardness filled the car. Zack had been influencing her, in more ways than she was comfortable with. He made her want to believe in fairy tales again. The comfort she felt with him around, the ease with which they spoke to each other—both made her want to try being worthy of love and understanding. "Whatever it is, I don't care as long as it helps us both get back to our own lives."

"Right." He clicked the blinker. "What's the water-front address from your sister's papers?"

Once she'd opened her backpack, she fished through the envelope until she found the page. "1971 Swanson Road."

"Do you have your phone handy?"

"I don't carry one. Too easy to track me."

When they stopped at a red light, Zack picked up his cell from the console and typed in his personal code. "Look up the directions and then read them to me."

Fifteen minutes later, Zack pulled off the main road into the Hampton Waterfront Complex. He drove slowly between two long strips of loading docks for a variety of businesses with address numbers. At the end of the drive was another building with Narragansett Bay drifting behind it.

"It's got to be that one." Jamie pointed toward the far end of the complex.

No cars sat beside the building. To the immediate right was the bay. To the left, a parking lot. Pulling up front would leave them exposed. He drove toward the back of the abandoned building where they found a loading dock. A small area for a handful of cars sat between the door and the bay. They'd be less likely to be found if he parked back here. "I don't know if I like this," Zack said.

"Ten minutes, tops," Jamie coaxed. "We'll be in and out." When he made no movement, she reached for the door handle. "Fine. Then wait here and I'll be back in a couple of minutes."

"No." He grabbed her arm. What happened if someone caught them breaking and entering? With one dumb decision, he could crush his career. Besides his family, it was all he had. "It doesn't feel right."

"Maybe not, but my sister wrote this address down. We need to know why."

"Let me go in," he suggested. At least she could drive away if needed.

She shook her head. "No. It's my future on the line and this could be a key element to helping me prove I was justified in taking my niece away."

Seconds ticked by.

He glanced at the time on his cell phone. "We go in, but if I tell you we're leaving, don't argue."

"But, Zack, we need to be thorough."

"Which won't help either of us if we get caught trespassing." He grabbed his duffel bag and searched for his lock-picking tools.

She bit her bottom lip.

"I can see the wheels spinning in your brain." Zack shook his head. "I'm not backing down on this. We go together and you follow my directions or we don't go at all."

A few more seconds breezed by. "All right. I won't argue with you."

As Jamie hurried out of the vehicle, Zack raised his hands and his gaze to the roof. Why did he not believe her?

Quickly he exited the vehicle and caught up with her. Seagulls squawked as they flew all around the bay. The water lapped lazily against the rocks, louder with each of their steps closer to the door.

What he wouldn't give to be anywhere else but in this parking lot.

Standing in front of it, the building looked rundown. Rust covered parts of the metal door and the upside down McGinty's Restaurant sign sat on the ground. An old window frame leaned against the wall. Graffiti decorated various sections of the metal. The lock on the door, though, was in mint condition. Yep, something valuable had to be in here.

Knots tightened in his gut. Normally he wouldn't approach a scene like this without proper backup. Jamie was cute and all, but for a possibly dangerous situation, he'd prefer one of his brothers or Jessa.

Jamie placed her hand on the door handle. Zack held her back. Slowly he approached the door and set his ear to the metal. The sounds of the bay surrounded them, but no noises came from inside the building. Once he'd unlocked the door, he slowly pushed it open and stepped inside.

The stench of mold assaulted him immediately, but Zack had learned to overcome smells of most kinds in his line of work. Behind him, Jamie blew out a breath of disgust. He scanned the room, which had to be the size of a YMCA. Large fluorescent lights hung suspended from the ceiling, slivers of light fell from high, rectangular windows, wooden boxes piled on top of each other in some parts of the room and sometimes standing alone.

He rushed to the first set of boxes. A shipping company's name stuck out through the plastic used for wrapping the box. Jamie pulled a piece of paper free. "What does it say?" he asked as he closed the distance between them.

"It matches the name on the side of the box and lists

ceramic items." As she folded the paper up, she added, "It also has an address."

When she shifted to push the paper into her pocket, Zack grabbed her wrist. "You're not taking that."

"It can be useful."

"You want to give your brother-in-law something else to hold against you?" He tugged his phone out of his pocket. "But here." He took a picture of the receipt. "We'll see what we can find out about the company." Then Jamie stuffed it back where she found it. Zack returned his attention to the box. To make the trip worthwhile, he needed to know if the contents of each box matched the invoices. He scanned the floor for something to crack the box open.

Jamie rushed to the next set of boxes. "Zack, over here." Before he reached her side, she shoved her hands inside the already opened box. Wiping away the dust and Bubble Wrap, she held up a ceramic cat with intricate details all over its body. Mrs. Cecily would love it.

Again, Jamie leaned into the box and switched out another ceramic item. He couldn't quite pinpoint what it was supposed to be. "These match the invoice." She frowned. "But I don't get it. What does any of this stuff have to do with Drew, my sister or Beth?"

"I think I know." Too many times in his career he'd uncovered drugs stashed inside household trinkets. What other reason would Timmins have for receiving three boxes of porcelain animals? "Drugs."

"Really?"

Zack pushed the contents of the box around, hoping to find anything to confirm his suspicions. A couple of the cats underneath had been broken, as though they'd been used to confirm the boxes' contents and then hidden at the bottom. Sure enough, inside were plastic packets of clear drugs. Bingo. He held up one packet.

"What is it?"

"Most likely crystal meth."

Jamie grabbed the packet and studied it. "So, the rumors are true. Drew's involved in selling drugs."

"All we have is an abandoned building with drugs inside. We don't know who owns the building or who's responsible for the boxes besides the shipping company on the invoices."

"Oh, we know." She handed the bag back to him.

"Yes, but we can't prove it yet." He reorganized the box to erase any proof of their visit.

Jamie's fingers danced along one of the animals. "Should we take one of the cats with us?"

"No. For one thing, we don't want Timmins to know we were here. Plus, if we were to get caught by the good authorities, I don't want drugs found in my sister's friend's vehicle. It definitely wouldn't look good for any—"

Faint voices drifted in through the windows. Zack's insides meshed together. He set his finger to his lips.

Jamie's eyes widened. Blood drained from her face.

Zack hurried to shift the box cover in place. His heart rate raced. He scrambled around to her side of the box, grabbed her and dropped to the floor. *Please, God, let me get us out of here alive and unharmed.*

The door opposite their entrance opened.

Jamie clamped her eyes shut and begged for the arriving people to be anyone but—

"In other words, we've got nothing new." Drew's voice stabbed into her ear.

*Dear God, if You're there, please get Zack and me to safety.*

When she opened her eyes, Zack crouched before her, cool, confident and calm...ish.

"Come on, Drew," George began. "We've found her once before. We'll do it again."

"Yeah, but before she makes my life even more complicated? She visited her sister so often, I wish she'd been at the house the day I shot Erin. Then I could've gotten rid of them both."

The man was talking about wanting to kill her. And he'd just admitted he murdered her sister.

Jamie clenched her teeth together. Rage filled her. He was her main reason to fight. The world around them deserved to know how horrendous Drew Timmins was.

Zack set a hand on her back and made miniature circles between her shoulder blades. His touch held her anger still.

"When's our next shipment coming in?" her brother-in-law asked.

"Monday."

"And these crates?" Drew asked.

When a rat or mouse squeaked as it crossed the room a few yards away, Jamie bit her tongue to keep from screaming. She inched closer to Zack, as though he were her knight in shining armor. But his sword was a rusted metal pipe a few feet from him.

"The guys are picking them up tonight and distributing them by tomorrow afternoon," George explained.

"How about our payment?"

"I'm meeting Charlie for supper tomorrow."

Footsteps thumped slowly across the floor. The sound of the shoes faded and the voices quieted to mumbles.

Zack inched his head around the corner of the box.

Jamie held her breath. When he turned back to her, he pointed over her shoulder toward the door they'd entered, mouthed something, then, with his hands, motioned her to move.

But Drew was so close. "Wait," she whispered as she held up her hands.

Zack's gaze turned to stone. Again, he pointed toward the wall behind her.

Yeah, she had agreed to follow his directions before they'd entered the building, but there'd be a small window of no coverage. Was it worth running? As she pointed to the floor, she mouthed the word *here*.

Zack scooted around her, grabbed her wrist and yanked her to her feet behind a pile of boxes.

They started for the door.

"Drew, hey! Over there!" George hollered.

Drew grabbed the back of her shirt collar. Jamie screamed. George passed her and slammed Zack into the wall. The sound of disturbed metal echoed through the building. Her heart crashed into her ribs. Her brother-in-law whirled her around. In her side vision, Zack took punch after punch and only threw a few of his own. Drew yanked her away from the other two men and banged her backside against the metal wall. With poisonous fire in his eyes, he wrapped his hand around her throat.

Panic set in. She clawed at his arm. Yes, at the moment she could still breathe, but the light pressure of each finger against her skin pushed away any sense of possible control she might have. "While your boyfriend gets his butt kicked, you will tell me what I want to know."

"You'll never get your daughter back." Her voice rasped.

"I will." He applied a bit more pressure with his fingers.

Zigzag designs filled her vision. She kept her mouth shut. Tried to keep as calm as possible. The sound of pounding punches tunneled in her ears.

"Tell me where you're hiding her." He tightened his hold.

Jamie looked right into his dark, evil eyes. She refused to show fear.

"Your confidence is…cute, but it won't last." He moved so close she could feel his coffee breath across her face. "*You* won't last."

How long could a person survive without air?

*Resist, resist, resist…*

Drew's fingers loosened a bit from Jamie's neck as he glanced around.

Jamie inhaled as much air as she could. Gathering what little strength she had, she jammed her knee into his body.

A string of swear words flew from his mouth as he doubled over. He howled. Then struggled to grasp her again.

She jerked away as Zack stood up straight. George lay on the ground. Was he dead? Had she turned Zack Owen, bounty hunter, into a killer? Her stomach rioted.

"Come on!" He grabbed her wrist and pulled her toward the door near their car. Jamie ran as fast as she ever had. Zack, she was sure, had slowed down so he could protect her from behind. Birds tweeted as though nothing had changed. Pockets of sun streaming through the darkening clouds covered her. But it wasn't a normal, safe day. Her brother-in-law had—

The metal door crashed against the building. She pushed herself harder. Her lungs burned, her heart knocked in her chest. She grabbed the car door handle and slid inside.

Drew and George yelled. They were close.

Then they disappeared back inside the building.

"Where'd they go?"

"Probably parked on the other side." Zack shoved the key in the ignition.

"Come on, Zack. Get us out of here."

"Working on it." The tires squealed as Zack reversed the vehicle.

Her heart kept beating rapidly. She and Zack passed the lawmen as they jumped into a nondescript sedan. No sheriff's car, no uniforms. They must be off duty. They peeled out of the parking space.

Zack sped up and rushed out the same way they'd entered the complex, through the strip of loading docks. In front of them, an eighteen-wheeler shifted into their path. Their vehicle wasn't slowing down. "Zack, what are you doing?"

"Losing our tail." He pushed the accelerator down. The vehicle approached the truck, veering to the slim empty space on the left between the front of the truck and a wall. The truck driver honked his horn.

*God, I know I don't deserve Your protection, but please keep us safe, for Zack.*

Another vehicle's horn sounded as it slipped diagonally into their path. The rig jerked to a halt. Zack pushed through the empty space and did a zigzag motion to escape the second vehicle.

She spun around to glance out the back window. Drew's car was stuck. "We're safe." Giddiness rumbled through her.

"Not yet." Zack glanced out his side mirror. He didn't slow the car as they rejoined the traffic.

They traveled in silence for several minutes while Zack took turn after turn and shifted through the traffic.

"What about the drugs? Shouldn't we call and report them?"

"Your brother-in-law will probably spin it so he and Linden look like they're doing an investigation and maybe even claim you're involved. Or they'll have cleared the place before the police even arrive."

"I hadn't thought of it that way."

He joined the traffic for I-95. "Now we're safe."

"That was too close." Jamie leaned against the seat, closed her eyes and willed her heart to slow down. She brushed her fingers across her neck. If she thought about it for too long, she could almost feel Drew's hand around her throat again.

No. She had to be strong. For Charlotte, for herself. For Zack, too? Yes, because she owed him.

Boy, the list of people she could potentially hurt kept growing. First Greta, the woman guarding Jamie's niece, then Charlotte and now Zack. To keep everyone safe dropped a serious amount of responsibility on her shoulders. Would she crumble under the weight again?

As they traveled along the highway, Zack kept to the speed limit and occasionally glanced in the rearview mirror to make sure the sedan wasn't in sight. Jamie kept quiet and stared out the passenger-side window. Did she see the clouds darkening in the distance? Or was her brain still on the moments when Timmins had her by the throat? Seeing her in such danger had caused two separate problems. One, Zack was distracted and got hit. A lot. Two, he felt helpless.

Like he had with his sick girlfriend and the store clerk who'd got injured because he'd allowed his emotions to interfere with his day job. He ground his teeth. This was exactly where he did not want to be. Hadn't he learned his lesson?

Jamie had looked so terrified pinned up against the wall. "Are you all right? Timmins didn't hurt you too much, did he?"

Strands of her hair covered her fingers as she brushed her hand along her neck. She kept her gaze outside. "I'm okay."

If they had watched the building and taken pictures instead of breaking and entering... No, that wouldn't have worked. They wouldn't know about the drugs and Timmins's plans to use them to make money. And they wouldn't have heard the sheriff's confession about killing his wife. Zack had trusted his gut that Jamie was telling the truth, but hearing the confirmation for himself changed the whole ball game.

He shook his head. Too much to think about, too much to be in charge of, and yet his conscience wouldn't let him just walk away. *Please, God, guide me in the right direction.*

When they reached the motel, Zack parked and turned off the ignition. Desperation waged a war within him. Pressure threatened to crush his shoulders. Relief made him want to weep. They'd come so close to...

He reached over, cupped Jamie's cheeks and kissed her. Her soft lips tasted like the sweetest dessert he'd ever had. Energy surged within him. Strands of her hair dangled over his fingers, drifting against his skin. Letting her go was not an option. Through his mouth, he begged to hold on to the connection, to know she still believed in him. They'd survived the most danger they'd experienced so far. Together.

She matched his intensity. Her palms pressed against his chest, not to push him away, but maybe to join with him on a different level. The warmth of her touch, the trust she surrendered bolted right for his heart. Maybe she did still have faith in him.

He pressed his forehead to hers. "I'm so sorry I wasn't able to protect you."

"But you did. You pulled me out of the real danger."

"Not without bruises." Because he'd failed her, he had no right to kiss her.

But he had. And he wanted to again.

No, he couldn't. His kiss had only been a reaction to the frightening events at the waterfront. Nothing more. He had no intention of pursuing a romance with Jamie, so his lips had no right being on hers.

He pulled back but took his time removing his hand from her face. He liked the way she remained tucked into his palm, her gentle lips barely touching his skin.

"We should go." They were sitting ducks in the parking lot.

Jamie sat up and pressed her fingertips to her lips. Almost instantly, her cheeks turned the color of spaghetti sauce. "You're right." Glancing down, she grabbed her backpack and exited the vehicle.

Great. He'd made her uncomfortable, and if he tried to soothe her, he might be coaxed into kissing her again. Granted it would be a wonderful cycle to be in, but his first priority, his *only* priority, had to be her safety. Nothing more.

Once he grabbed his duffel bag and caught up to her, they climbed the cement stairs to their second-floor motel rooms. Tomorrow they'd have to check out and move to another motel. When his skips were on the run, they often didn't stay in the same place more than a night or two. Remaining here any longer wouldn't be safe.

Jamie's hands shook as she opened her motel room door. Residual effects of Timmins's assault or of their kiss?

Once inside her room, Jamie rushed to take a seat at the table. As though blocking him out, she covered her face with her hands. Zack twisted the locks and set the chain in place.

Through the doorway, voices hollered from somewhere close by. Outside the window, drops of rain hit the glass like tiny beads. A rumble of thunder cracked through the sky. A heavy coat of tension filled the room. His inner voice ordered him to move. He grabbed his phone out of his duffel, sat in the other chair and dialed his big brother's phone number.

"Kyle, we could really use your help," he said as soon as his brother picked up.

Silence brought about heightened nerves. Zack wasn't sure what he'd do if his family wouldn't back him now.

"Are you two okay?"

What a loaded question. Zack glanced over to Jamie, who still had her face hidden.

"Zack? Are you in danger?" Worry laced his brother's voice.

"No, we're safe at the moment."

"All right, then." After a deep breath, Kyle continued, "Tell me what's going on."

"This sheriff is bad news. Jamie was right about him."

"Do you have any specific evidence?"

"None that will hold up in court, not yet."

"But…"

"He's selling drugs and admitted to killing Jamie's sister."

"Do I want to know how you know that?" Zack could almost see his brother sitting in his office chair, massaging his forehead.

"Probably not, but you need to hear it all."

Zack shared everything he and Jamie had come across since leaving the Second Chance office yesterday. He admitted to asking Jessa and Lily for assistance. Then he listened to his brother's instructions.

Kyle had reluctantly taken over the father-figure role when their own dad died. He'd been the strength of the family and Zack couldn't be more thankful to be back in his brother's good graces.

When he set the phone on the table, Jamie turned to face him. Her arms remained crossed. "What's the verdict? Will they help us now?"

"Yeah." He nodded. "With all we've uncovered, Kyle believes I was justified in breaking you out of jail. He's going to ask our friend Logan, who's a detective, to look into Timmins and Linden off the record. Jessa's going to find out whatever she can about Beth's disappearance. Once we go through the list of men on the other piece of paper from your sister's envelope, I'll call Kyle back and he and Parker will decide what to do next. In the meantime, they're going to look into the McGinty's building and find out who owns it."

"And your sister?"

"She's manning the office. We don't usually include Lily in anything that could potentially put her in trouble."

"But you do with Jessa?"

"Jessa's a trained agent. My sister's not."

Jamie nodded as she looked out the window. Her fingers drifted to her neck, caressing the spot where Timmins had tried to choke her. The look of despair shrouding her eyes cut like a knife through his insides. Add to it the guilt she forced on her own back... Oh, what he wouldn't give to spend five minutes alone with Drew Timmins.

No. He had to trust in God to take care of Timmins. Maybe Zack could coach Jamie into trusting the Father, too. Maybe that assignment was why He put Zack and Jamie together. Honestly, he couldn't think of any other reason why he felt so connected to her.

Zack set his hands on the table, palms facing up. "Give me your hands."

Without hesitation, she complied. The instant trust, for a change, warmed him. He curled his fingers around hers and lowered his head. "Father, please give us both strength and guide us on the path You've chosen for us. Help soothe Jamie's heart and restore the hope I see in her eyes so often. Help me make good decisions to keep us both safe. Amen."

"You pray for me?"

She hadn't pulled her hands away so he kept hold of her delicate fingers. "Believe it or not, I've kept you in my prayers since we met."

"Why?"

"Why not?" He rubbed his thumbs along her skin.

"I was doing all right, Zack, keeping it together, but after today, after finding out so much more about Drew, then the run-in…" She closed her eyes for a few seconds, took a deep breath and then released it. "In my life, I'm supposed to be able to anticipate and fix problems before they become a big deal. As a teacher, it's what I'm trained for, what I'm good at. But in this illegal and dangerous world, my skills fall very short. With each hour that passes, I feel less in control and less likely to ever get it back."

"I don't know what to tell you, Jamie. I'm doing the best I can."

"I know and I'm not blaming you."

"Think twice before you say that. I almost got you seriously hurt."

"No, you didn't." She pulled her hand free and set her soft fingers on the side of his face. "Drew did. You stopped him. It may not have worked out as you wanted, but in the end, we both got away. I couldn't have asked for anything more."

The scent of woman drifted off her skin and messed with his head. Her faith in him made him want to be... good enough.

But being good enough at his job took all his effort. Getting caught up in a woman would mess with his focus, and he wouldn't jeopardize anyone's safety for foolish desires. No relationship was worth the risk.

Although, this woman, a person he was supposed to be hunting, continued to open up little chunks of his heart. While his gaze drifted to her mouth, his brain remembered the intensity of their kiss. As much as he wanted to, though, he couldn't kiss her again. It wouldn't be fair to either of them. They could never be a couple. Yet the time they spent together made him think... What if he decided to take a chance?

He reached down and pulled his laptop out of his duffel bag. "We should figure out what our next step is."

Zack might be ready to move on, but the memory of his lips against hers, the gentle touch he used to caress her cheeks, had Jamie's brain locked around their kiss. It had been better than she'd thought it could be, better than any kiss she'd shared before. Of course, it wasn't about the actual kiss, although that had been wonderful enough. More important, she loved how he made her feel—strong, beautiful, cherished. The whole experience left her longing for more.

But she wasn't a kid anymore and acting like a lovesick teenager was not acceptable. She had to focus on what was most important in her life—her niece and convicting Drew. Not romance.

She pulled the journal from her backpack. Thunder crackled. A stab of lightning lit up the sky. She sifted through the pages for the paper with the list of men's names, then moved closer to Zack. *Don't look at him. Ignore the subtle shift in our relationship.* "Let's look up these names. Maybe we can figure out how they're connected."

"Sounds good." He pulled up the internet. "Okay, who's first?"

As heavier rain hit the windows, Jamie scanned the sheet. "Roger Travis."

Zack's fingers flew over the keys. Soon a newspaper article popped up on the screen. "He died downtown in Providence two years ago. Shot by a drug dealer. Next name."

"Jeff Otis."

He pulled up an obituary. "Died six months ago."

"Okay, next one is—"

"Wait." He typed away and pulled up a website called atn.com. "We use this site called All That's Needed to gather information about our clients. Sometimes we get clues from family, friends and neighbors, but ATN gives us more, like their arrest record, threat assessment, social media, outcomes of court appearances, cause of death if they're no longer with us." When he typed in Otis's name, a long list of offenses filled the screen. "Says he died of a drug overdose. Next name."

She scanned the list. "Dan Butler."

Zack searched again. ATN had no information on Mr. Butler so Zack widened the search to the rest of the internet. On the state newspaper website came a picture of a man in a long-sleeved shirt and dress pants. A bunch of little kids sat on a wooden floor watching him and someone in a dog costume. "Finally, a good guy." Jamie inched closer and read the caption.

"Do you see what all three of these men have in common?" He leaned against the back of his chair.

She shook her head. "What?"

"Drugs."

"The third man, though, wasn't dealing or doing drugs. He was teaching children to stay away from them."

"Still connected." Zack glanced at the next name on the list and typed it into their search. A link to Hampton's small town newspaper popped up. In a tiny paragraph written five years ago was a story about this man arrested with a huge load of crystal meth in his car.

Zack tapped the paper in her hands. "When I look up these other names, I'll almost guarantee they'll also be involved with drugs in some way."

They could look up the criminal background of these men, find out how many of them were still alive, where they might be and how they could be connected to Drew or his deputies.

Zack glanced at the next name and then started typing again.

"Wait. Let me have the pen." She reached across the keyboard and grabbed it. Setting the list of names on the table, she prepared to write. "I'll jot down a few words for each name so we know what happened with each man."

Zack nodded. "Then we'll have more information for Kyle and the others to help us with."

Together they worked for another hour taking notes, discussing each man's past and examining how their findings in the warehouse by the water tied into the list of names. In the midst of all this, Parker called to say that when he and Jessa arrived at the warehouse, there were still some boxes there, but no drugs were inside. Just like Zack's prediction as they were driving back to their motel.

Jamie rubbed her eyes, planted her arms on the table's surface and then set her chin on the back of her hands. "We have ten names on here. Four of these men are dead, three of them are involved in Drew's Don't Do Drugs program for public schools, two of them are 'responsible, reformed citizens' after some jail time and one guy, Teddy Copeland, is still in prison."

"And every single one of them is connected to Timmins."

She tapped her fingers on the table and stared out at the dark sky. "Plus, we've got Beth's car accident and disappearance. We now have more information about Drew's illegal activities but still no concrete evidence to support our theories."

"Don't get discouraged." He pressed his palm on her back and made tiny circular movements that rubbed away some of her stress. "Plus, we're not alone anymore. We've got my family behind us."

"I can't tell you what a relief it is to know some people actually believe me."

"It'll work out. Soon everyone will know how crooked Timmins is and you and your niece will be free from his reach."

"How can you be so positive all the time?"

He shrugged. "I know I have God on my side. He won't ever give me more than I can handle."

She smiled. "I wish I had your faith."

"Were you not raised to love God?"

"We were. But I started to question my faith when my parents were killed. I prayed for strength. Then when Erin married Drew, I prayed for God to turn Drew's heart to love instead of possession. When I saw how violent he was becoming, I prayed Erin would come to her senses. When she finally did, I wasn't around to help her. I let her down, and in doing so I let Him down. Then He took my sister. After Erin died, I didn't see the point of having faith anymore."

"God didn't take your sister, Jamie. Timmins shot her."

"God allowed it to happen."

Zack opened his mouth but must've thought better about what he'd planned to say. Silence overtook the room until a crack of thunder broke through. Zack set his arms on his thighs and clasped his hands. "You want to know what I think?"

"Yes." It surprised her how much she really did. As they'd talked, about the case and about life in general, she'd started to value his thoughts and opinions.

"I think your sister would be proud of you for taking such good care of your niece and for fighting to make sure Timmins pays for his crimes."

She shook her head. "I don't know if I agree with you."

Ignoring her, he continued, "And I know for a fact God hasn't given up on you. He still loves you and wants to be part of your life."

"How can you be so sure?"

"Faith." He lifted his hand toward her face as though to cup her cheek, but he lowered his arm just as quickly.

A heavy blanket of regret covered every inch of her. She fought to keep from maneuvering into Zack's arms. She needed his physical comfort more now than any other time with him, but he couldn't give it for whatever reason. Tears began to gather in the corners of her eyes. She would not cry in front of him.

She stood. "Zack, I'm really tired." She walked to the door between their rooms. "If you don't mind, I'd like to go to bed early tonight." She opened the door for him. So much had happened in the last twelve hours her brain was fried. And having him near her wasn't as soothing right now. Yes, she still trusted him with her safety, but her emotions swirled like a tornado. She had no desire for him to witness the disaster.

He grabbed his computer and his duffel bag, then stepped into his own room. "Good night, Jamie. Sleep well."

"You, too." She closed the door behind him.

With all the thoughts swarming in her mind, she hoped she could.

The thunder and lightning had stopped, but Jamie still tossed and turned. The clock's green lights read 11:22. She plopped a pillow over her head. Yes, she was tired, but her brain wouldn't stop working. After she'd let Erin down, she hadn't been sure she deserved any support.

Could God have other ideas? He had brought Zack to her campsite, right? And Zack had been her number one supporter on so many levels ever since. Maybe God was working for her but just not how she'd wanted or expected.

Another part of her feared Zack's presence too much. He'd kissed her and she'd liked it, enjoyed the positive feelings his presence brought to her life. A zillion reasons not to kiss him swam through her mind, yet… Zack

Owen was not an easy man to resist. But would God send him away and leave her alone? Again? She wouldn't blame Him. Jamie had no right expecting—

A jiggling noise yanked her out of her thoughts. She stilled. Glanced at the door to the concrete pathway outside. Another jiggling noise.

She jerked upright. Tension coursed through her. She looked toward the door between her room and Zack's. Light under the door. He was up. He'd hear her.

Her bedroom door flew open. Her heart rate spiked. Two men rushed forward. She scrambled across the bed toward the doorknob, to her partner. "Help me!"

The stench of sweat and evil overwhelmed her senses. One man grabbed her under the armpits as the other man took hold of her ankles. She fought, twisting and wiggling and screaming as much as she could. Once she got her feet free, she brought them back up and kicked the man as hard as she could. "Zack!"

# SEVEN

Zack scrambled out of the chair he occupied and ran to the door. Thumping and screaming chilled him to the bone. "Jamie!" He yanked open the door to her room and flipped the light switch by the main entrance. The two men who'd attacked them at her campsite held her, one at her feet, the other at her shoulders. She punched, kicked and bit as much as she could.

The man with her feet, the smaller of the two, dropped them and stalked toward Zack. Zack was ready for him, though, bending to avoid the sloppy cross punch and delivering a swift punch to the man's stomach. A few jabs and a solid uppercut took the guy out.

One down, one to go.

Zack looked up. The other guy had one arm wrapped around Jamie's chest. This man was Chad, Chuck, Charlie. She continued to fight him as he dragged her toward the doorway. Zack moved forward. "Hey!" He gripped the second man's collar and wrenched him backward. He punched him in the side once, twice. The man only flinched, but the movement was enough for Jamie to break free.

Zack punched again. And again. After his opponent threw a cross, Zack slammed him against the open door.

A loud crash sounded from across the room. Panic rushed through him. Jamie! He searched for her by the desk.

Pride crushed his fear. She stood over the still body of the second guy. What had she used to knock—

The big, beefy man in front of him jammed both fists into Zack's gut. He bent at the waist and fought for a full breath. Another punch landed across his jaw. After a quick prayer, Zack punched back—the stomach, the side, the face twice. Still more punches. Again, he smacked the guy into the wall, but this time the man didn't come back. Instead, his body slid down and landed like a rag doll on the floor. Two intruders. Both out cold.

"Zack?" Jamie appeared in the doorway between their rooms with his duffel bag in her hand. Hanging off her shoulder was her backpack.

He rushed forward, pressed his hands to her temples and kissed her forehead. "Good job."

In the distance, sirens came to life. "Come on." He took his duffel and grabbed her hand. "We've got to get out of here." He hurried her into the muggy night air and down the cement stairs to the parking lot. A couple of times she glanced back to their rooms. Worrying those guys had revived? If yes, then that made two of them. He picked up his speed.

On the driver's side of their current vehicle, he jingled the keys to find the correct one. "Jamie, get over to the passenger side," he directed.

She didn't move. Her hands remained twisted in the fabric of his shirt. From the motel, more voices yelled.

"Do you think it's them?" Fear laced her words.

"Don't know." A high dose of energy pushed him. He opened the door. The window by his elbow shattered.

"Get down!" He crouched behind the door and covered Jamie. Her whole body shook. Screams competed with the police sirens to fill the air.

A bullet, then a second, slammed into Zack's door. "Get in and crawl across. Keep your head down." He shoved her, the backpack and his duffel into the car.

As soon as he could, he scooted into the driver's seat, started the car and backed out of the parking space. The door fell loosely into place. He threw the gearshift into Drive and tore out of the parking lot.

For several miles, he kept his gaze shifting between the rearview mirror and the road in front of them. They were able to travel far and fast enough to avoid a tail. Still, he'd be vigilant. He'd managed to evade the crooked authorities again, but if he kept pushing it he'd eventually lose. Especially because the more time he spent with her, the more attached to Jamie's well-being he became.

Warm air floated across the side of his face, in from the broken window. As he drove through the city, his heartbeat retreated closer to normal. With a quick glance across the vehicle, he assessed the woman who kept impacting his life. His duffel sat on the floor between her feet. In her lap, she gripped her backpack like a lifeline. Her gaze never strayed from the windshield.

"Jamie?" She didn't respond. He reached out, his fingertips brushing over her knuckles.

She jerked toward the passenger door while her shell-shocked expression turned to him.

"We're okay." Was he trying to convince her or himself? Or both of them?

A nod was her only response.

He kept driving until he saw a busy nightclub. After turning into the parking lot, Zack drove to the back of the building. Loud hip-hop music blasted out of the club's windows. As many cars sat in this parking lot as the one in front, which was perfect.

He slipped the gear into Park and turned off the engine. *Please, God, give me the right words to soothe her.*

Jamie studied the building in front of them. "Why are we here? I don't drink and I couldn't eat anything if I wanted to." What was he thinking? At a time like this, they had to get as far away from the motel as possible. Knots filled her stomach and too many emotions whirled through every inch of her. Charlie and Ben could be within minutes of her and Zack's location, ready to shoot at them again. Tears burned the corners of her eyes.

"We're not going inside. I wanted somewhere for our car to blend in for a few minutes."

"Oh." The leaves of the trees surrounding the parking area swayed in the breeze.

The harsh words of her potential kidnappers still rang in her ears. The strength of Charlie's grip remained etched into her body. She nipped her bottom lip. She would not cry.

Zack cupped her chin, his touch warm and strong and comforting. Jamie closed her eyes for a moment. For the first time since the thugs broke into her room, she took a steady breath.

"You're safe." His thumb brushed over her cheek. With each movement of Zack's finger, a bit more of her panic slipped away. "Take a deep breath and let it out slowly." Like a teacher, he guided her through several breaths until her heart rate had almost returned to normal.

"Thank you." She should pull her head free, but honestly, she craved the comfort only Zack could give her.

After all they'd faced tonight, she could take a few more minutes of compassion.

"I could almost see my life flashing before my eyes. I thought they were going to kill me."

Too soon, Zack removed his hand. "Not likely. You're too important."

"And you're not?"

"To Timmins? No. They want to keep you alive long enough to tell them where Charlotte is." He pointed to himself. "Me, on the other hand, they have no use for."

"How can you say that?"

"Timmins is smart enough to know if he names me as an accomplice and pushes to get me arrested, my family and I will fight back. By keeping me off the radar, he can claim I got caught in the cross fire if they catch us. Then he gets exactly what he wants—you in custody and me dead."

"He also thinks he's too important and no one can touch him," Jamie added.

"Right."

"I'm sorry for putting you into the line of fire." If it weren't for her, his world wouldn't be flipped upside down.

He glanced outside the windshield. "At least we know one new thing now."

"What?"

Several people stepped out the back door of the club. The music blasted until the metal door slammed shut. Quiet chatter began as tiny orange lights appeared.

"We're rattling the cage. My guess is Timmins never expected you to be so much of a challenge for him."

She nodded. "I can't figure out how they found us at the motel. We're not even in their jurisdiction."

He shrugged. "Well, the mail center clerk had seen you somewhere, maybe on TV. Someone from the motel might've seen you on the news, too, and decided they wanted to see justice done. Or get a reward." Zack rubbed his fingers over the steering wheel. "Sometimes we pay motel employees and guests to deliver criminals to us. You'd be amazed at what people will do for a few dollars. Maybe Timmins's men forked over cash for our location. He has a lot of guys on his payroll. He could've had any or all of them scouring motels for us."

The stench of cigarettes cruised through their windows. "But why wait until tonight to come after us?"

"Think about it. Most people need a few minutes to feel human when they get up in the morning. If we're woken up in the middle of the night, there's more of a chance to keep us confused, get rid of me and take you back to your brother-in-law."

"But we stopped them." She allowed herself to smile.

"Yes, we did. You did pretty good back there." He leaned against the door. "When I first found you in Timmins's jail cell, you were scared and hurt. When I decided to take you out of there, I thought my brothers and I would be the ones doing all the work to solve the case."

A soft chuckle escaped his lips, which made her smile grow bigger. The tightly squeezed knots in her chest began to loosen.

"I never thought you could put up a fight like you did in the motel, and knocking out the second guy? Wow. What did you hit him with?"

"The first thing I thought of. The lamp. I yanked the cord out of the wall and slammed it into his head as hard as I could."

"Remind me not to make you angry." Zack laughed.

"I don't think that can happen."

"Oh, trust me it can. Ask anyone in my family."

Silence took over between them. Colored lights flashed through the windows of the club. The smokers finished their cigarettes and reentered the building.

"What do we do now, Zack?"

"Figure out another place to hide. Everywhere we could go is a risk. I don't want to go to any of my family's places and put them in any more danger than we've already put them in by asking for help. If we go to another motel in Rhode Island, someone may recognize you again and contact the police. We could go over the Massachusetts border and stay in a motel there. But we'll switch locations each night so we'll be harder to track."

The man had saved her life, more than once. He encouraged her when she was overwhelmed. He never treated her like a failure and he was still by her side despite the times she'd argued with him. Wasn't it time for her to put all of her trust in him? "I know a place we can go."

His eyes widened. His mouth opened but no words came out.

"I need to see my niece and we need a safer place far away from here."

"Are you sure?"

"You said it yourself—she might have some information we could use to get justice for my sister." She nodded. "Yeah, it's time you met Charlotte."

By the time they pulled into a carport in Greta Corlen's apartment complex, the moon had moved a good distance across the sky. Sunrise was still a few hours away, though. Jamie had yawned incessantly, but she'd remained awake to give Zack directions to the Attleboro apartment and to keep him attentive with her chatter.

All along the journey, questions plagued her. Was this a good idea? Was she pulling Greta and Charlotte onto danger's road? She hadn't visited since going on the run strictly to keep them both safe. Drew and George had found Zack and her many times. Would they find them again?

Jamie shook the doubts from her mind. For now, they were safely away from Drew and his cohorts. No one in Massachusetts would be looking at her like a fugitive. Plus, Zack's family would keep up the search for clues.

As Jamie guided Zack toward her friend's front door, she grabbed his arm. "Wait. You have to understand Greta will be suspicious of you and Charlotte is a fragile little girl. You might scare her. Just please be careful with them both."

He opened his mouth to respond, but apparently changed his mind. Instead, he nodded.

Jamie knocked the appropriate number of times, waited a moment, then knocked again. After a few seconds, the locks turned and the door opened. "Jamie?" Greta's gaze shifted to Zack. "Is something wrong?"

In a lot of ways, Greta Corlen was the third Carter child. The woman had been friends with Jamie since second grade, had suffered through middle school with her and had joined Jamie in a high school faith program. And despite Jamie's difficult journey after her parents were killed, Greta hadn't left her side. They'd lost touch after high school graduation, but Greta had jumped at the chance to help with Charlotte after Erin's death.

Murder.

"We need a place to regroup and we have new questions for Charlotte." She fiddled with the strap of her backpack.

Greta pulled the door wider and ushered them into the apartment. As she closed and locked the door, she asked, "Is this really safe?"

"Probably not." She turned to her friend. "Greta, this is Zack Owen. He's a bounty hunter."

Greta narrowed her gaze on her. "Jamie."

"He broke me out of Drew's jail. I wouldn't have brought him here if I didn't trust him."

Greta nodded. "All right." She tossed her long braid over her shoulder and pulled Jamie into a hug. Once she released her, she turned to Zack. "Welcome to my home." She led them into the living room. The scent of cinnamon drifted into the air from a candle on the coffee table. A box of toys sat next to the television.

"Were you already up?"

Greta crossed her arms. "Yes. I'm having trouble sleeping again. So I've been reading for about an hour." The Bible Jamie had given Greta for her sixteenth birthday rested on one side of the couch. "What's happened that brought you here?"

Zack set his duffel bag on the floor. "Someone found us at the motel we were in and tried to take us out." He brushed his fingers along her shoulder as he tugged her backpack off. The movement was simple, innocent. Except with Zack, it added to her growing feelings for him. No matter what happened around them, he always treated her like she was...valuable.

Greta gasped. "What?"

Jamie squeezed her friend's hands. "We're all right." Maybe she'd wait a while before dropping the bomb about how much trouble she and Zack had gotten into. "How's Charlotte?"

"She's fine. She misses you, though."

Guilt crept inside Jamie's heart. Yes, she spent time away from her niece, but it was for a good reason. Unfortunately, the six-year-old might not understand it. "I need to see her."

"Of course." Greta smiled as she tightened the belt on her off-white robe. "Zack, why don't you fill me in on your time with Jamie while I make us some coffee."

"Sounds like a plan." Zack followed her into the kitchen.

Jamie wandered down the hallway and slowly opened the door to Greta's guest room. Charlotte lay in the center of the double bed, clutching the dilapidated stuffed elephant that never left her side. She'd been sending the toy down the slide when Jamie approached her in the park a few days after Erin's death. The scents of lotion and crayons drifted up to her nostrils as she stepped inside the room.

Jamie's heart relaxed. Her niece was safe. It took all her effort to keep from running to the bed and pulling the girl into her arms. Instead she crouched down beside the bed and brushed back Charlotte's bangs.

Jamie leaned forward and planted a kiss on the girl's forehead. Tomorrow morning she'd be able to hold her for as long as she wanted. "And with Zack's help, soon I won't have to leave you at all."

Zack woke to the smell of coffee brewing and something poking him in the arm. He opened one eye and found a short person standing next to him with one tiny finger extended. In her other hand, she held a stuffed pink elephant that had seen better days. "Good morning. I'm Charlotte. What's your name?"

"Zack." He shifted to lying on his side and yawned. She was a cute kid with long dark hair, hazel eyes and a smile with two perfectly spaced dimples. They must run in the family.

Sunlight peeked through the living room windows. Low whispers drifted in from the kitchen. He glanced at his watch. Seven thirty. Had he really slept longer than anyone else? "Good to meet you, Charlotte." He held out his hand to the little girl. How old was she? Six? Seven?

She shook his hand. "Auntie says you're our friend."

"That's right."

"Are you gonna help keep us safe?" She gnawed on the finger she'd poked him with.

"Absolutely."

"Good. I don't want Auntie Jamie to be scared anymore."

She held on to the stuffed animal with a death grip. The smile of curiosity she'd had when she first woke him changed quickly to a serious expression of concern. No doubt the kid knew more than either of the women gave her credit for.

"I'm going to do whatever I can to help her." He leaned forward, winked. "And you, too."

"Charlotte," Jamie whispered from the other room. "Don't bother Mr. Zack."

"It's all right. I'm up." He tossed the blanket across the back of the couch and set his feet on the floor. A cupboard door opened and closed. Something hit the countertop.

"I'm sorry." The little girl's frown messed with his insides.

"Don't worry about it."

Jamie wandered into the room and handed him a mug of steaming coffee.

"You're a lifesaver. Thanks." He accepted the cup and took a sip.

"Charlotte's just really inquisitive, especially with new people around."

"Not a problem." The first sip of the day always determined how his next twenty-four hours would go. The day he broke her out of jail, he'd burned the roof of his mouth. This sip released the taste of roasted almonds and coasted smoothly down his throat.

Jamie stood with a flowery skirt that reached her ankles and a solid white fancy T-shirt. Her hair, with the still-damp look, held a wave to it. She wore very little makeup. Suddenly a picture of the two of them walking barefoot along the beach popped into his head. What would it be like to entwine their fingers and wander with no worries…

He shook his head. Yes, he wanted her and the little one to be free, but he wouldn't be following along for the ride once they'd straightened out Jamie's warrant. He'd already started caring too much for Jamie, enjoying their precious moments of normalcy. But they were becoming friends, weren't they? Friends cared about one another without sliding into an emotional tumble that interfered with real life. Right?

The girl grabbed hold of Jamie's thigh with her hand and glanced up. "Auntie Jamie, can we go to the park and play on the playground?"

"Not today. I'm sorry." She leaned down and kissed the kid on the top of her head. "Mr. Zack and I have some work to do."

"Work that has to do with Daddy?"

"Yes, baby."

"Charlotte, breakfast is ready," Greta called from the kitchen.

"Come on, Auntie." She took hold of Jamie's hand and tugged her around the couch. "Are you coming, too, Mr. Zack?"

"Are you kidding? I wouldn't miss it." He patted his stomach. "I'm starving."

Once they'd finished eating, Jamie changed Charlotte out of her pajamas. Greta offered to take Charlotte to play with her plastic dollhouse in the guest room as long as Jamie joined them when she could.

An idea about what to do today popped into his head, one he was pretty sure was safe enough to encourage. But would Jamie be willing to trust him to make the decision? She'd gotten better about compromising with him. Maybe this time she'd see the sense in his reasoning from the start.

"Sorry about taking so much time for breakfast." Jamie stood next to him, set his duffel on the kitchen table and pulled his computer free. "Charlotte and I have spent so little time together since my sister's death I had to indulge her."

"Don't apologize for wanting to spend time with your niece." Teacher, crime fighter, attractive woman, friend, aunt. Jamie had so many layers to her and Zack wanted to uncover them all. He would love a chance to hang out with her when no one threatened her and her niece's lives. Sure, he and Jamie had spent some time over the last few days talking about things outside of her warrant and their hunt for evidence against Timmins, but Zack wanted more. He had a feeling they'd have a lot of fun together.

Her eyes shone bright this morning. "Thank you." She tucked her hair behind both ears. "But I know we need to—"

He pressed the pad of one finger to her lips. "You need to focus on your role as auntie and friend." And as a woman with no worries. She looked so pretty dressed in clothes she must've borrowed from Greta instead of the drab, generic ones he'd gotten her the other day.

A red tinge covered her cheeks. From his touch? The fact that he affected her as much as he did made him smile. It meant he wasn't the only one altered by their growing connection. He cupped her cheek. "You are beautiful, inside and out. You know that, right?"

Her gaze shifted up to meet him. A sliver of hope swarmed through her eyes. She set her small fingers on his wrist, not to tug him away, but as though she needed his strength. Sure, he could be strong for her, couldn't he? Friends supported each other all the time.

He carefully pulled his hand away. "You may not like what I'm going to tell you, but it's not up for discussion."

She rolled her eyes. "Zack, come on."

"No." He shook his head. "I'm going to interview Teddy Copeland."

"He's the only guy on Erin's list who's still in jail, right?"

"Yeah. Now here's the part you're not going to like. I'm going alone."

Jamie planted her hands on her hips, torn between her duty to prove Drew needed to be in prison and her duty to care for her niece. Both choices had consequences. But Zack heading to Wyndom Prison alone?

"No. Absolutely not. This is my fight, too." What if

she had questions for the man that Zack didn't ask? Or what if he kept some of the information he received to himself to *protect* her?

"Jamie." He set his hands on her shoulders. "Your niece needs you. You need your niece. You're staying here." He fished through the pockets of his cargo pants. "I'll be back in a couple of hours and I promise to tell you everything Copeland says."

She crossed her arms tight. "Will the prison just let you walk in and talk to this guy?"

"I figured I'd use my badge." He held it up. "I'll have to see the warden and get approval, but it shouldn't be a problem." He put on his lanyard, which held his Fugitive Recovery Agent badge.

She fingered the circular piece of metal that had an intricate design of an American flag draped around an eagle. "What if something happens to you?" Then she'd be on her own again.

Zack shook his head. "Nothing'll happen. Besides, I'm a bounty hunter, remember? I've been in prisons with my work. It's not a big deal."

His explanation made sense, but her emotions still whirled around within her. She'd spent so much time with him over the last few days it would be odd to be without him, even for only a few hours.

Good grief. If he evoked this much devotion from her now, what would she be like when they finally went their separate ways?

Charlotte's laughter sailed down the hallway.

Enough about herself. Jamie had to remember her fight. Her niece deserved to grow up unafraid and it was Jamie's responsibility to see that happen. "Where is Wyndom Prison?"

"Outside of Woonsocket, about forty-five minutes away."

"So you're going back to Rhode Island." She fingered the buttons on his shirt. "Is there anything I can do for us here?"

"Yeah." With his grin that always stirred the butterflies in her belly, he pointed toward the guest room. "Play with your niece." Zack grabbed keys from the counter and headed for the door. "Then check the news for any reports about us."

"Got it." She couldn't help but smile. *Us*. Like they were a couple. In some sense, they were. "A couple of crime fighters," she mumbled.

"Huh?" He glanced back to her.

Heat spread through her cheeks. She waved him off. "Nothing. Talking to myself. Is it safe to take the same car we've been driving?"

"Greta gave me her keys when you were getting Charlotte dressed."

When he pulled the front door open, she touched his arm. "Be careful. Come back to us." Right away, she squashed the terrible thoughts of her having to keep running without him. Yes, she preferred making decisions herself, but Zack had been the perfect temporary partner for her.

"You may not remember I'm a grown man." He winked. "I can handle one inmate."

Oh, yes, she had noticed. His black hair, his relentless determination, his day-old stubble, his fit body and his strong will. Siding with her was one handsome grown man. He was a perfect match for her world.

Except he wasn't really part of her world.

But…what would it be like to wake up with a man

like him in the house each day? To share coffee with him before Charlotte woke up each morning? To watch him carry her niece on his shoulders?

Wouldn't it be just like God to dangle Zack in front of her, then yank him away when she'd gotten used to having him around?

Then again, maybe God had brought Zack into her life to fan the tiny bit of hope buried deep inside her chest. Tight knots shooed out the butterflies in her stomach.

Charlotte babbled about some cartoon character as she and Greta walked into the kitchen. "Go on," Greta interrupted. "Grab your juice box from the refrigerator."

While Charlotte followed directions, Greta stood beside Jamie. "Did your friend leave?"

"Yeah. Running on another lead."

"How come you're not going with him?"

"We both decided I should stay here and play with Charlotte for a while."

Greta narrowed her gaze. She'd always been able to see the story behind the story.

"Okay, he decided but I agreed."

The fridge door shlurped closed. "Here. I got one for everybody." The little girl juggled four drinks as she walked over to Jamie and Greta.

"Thank you." Jamie took the drink, bent down and kissed her niece.

She beamed with pride as she handed over Greta's drink. With the other two in her hands, she glanced around the kitchen. "Where's Mr. Zack?"

"He had to go to work," Jamie said.

"Is he coming back?"

"Not till later, kiddo." Jamie tousled Charlotte's hair. "Why don't you return his drink to the refrigerator?"

Her eyes lit up. "Yeah, then he can have it when he comes home." With a bounce in her step, she walked to the fridge.

Jamie's friend of sixteen years smiled as she stared at Jamie.

"What?" she asked, although she knew the exact thoughts rushing through her friend's head. Greta was a romantic at heart and could always tell when Jamie had feelings for someone. Heat pushed up into her cheeks.

Oblivious to the women's silent communication, Charlotte skipped toward the front door. "Can we go to the playground?"

"Sure, sweetheart." Greta grabbed her house keys and guided Charlotte outside. Jamie took a sip from the juice box and followed behind them. Once Jamie and Greta sat down at a patio table by the community playground, her friend began, "Zack's a good, handsome man. They're hard to find. And he obviously cares about you."

Jamie shook her head. "There's nothing between Zack and me."

Greta bumped shoulders with Jamie. "But there could be."

Memories of their kiss whirled through her thoughts. Jamie couldn't help but smile. "He's very kind and funny." With a big sigh, she continued, "The kiss was great, too."

"Oh, you've kissed?"

She covered her face with her palm. "Yes, but it doesn't mean anything serious. He and I are so different and I have no time for a romantic relationship."

"You will when Drew is in prison."

"No, then my focus will be on Charlotte. I have to do right by her, for Erin."

"Yes, you have your niece to take care of, but you are allowed to have a life, too." Greta sipped her juice.

"Am I?"

"Of course. You deserve love as much as anyone else." Greta had never been one to hold her tongue. After shrugging, she continued, "And maybe Zack's in your life to remind you just how worthy of love you are."

Hope. Greta always gave it to Jamie, no matter what was going on around them. Jamie draped her arm over her friend's shoulders and hugged her tight. "You're a blessing to us, Greta. Thank you."

"A blessing?" Her friend's eyes brightened. "Have you started your path back to God?"

"I don't know." Had Zack influenced her? "Maybe."

Charlotte ran to the table and set her drink down. "Auntie Jamie, come play with me." Without waiting, she skipped back to the swing set. "Greta can push us both!"

The carefree call of her niece loosened the tension out of her shoulders. She may not be ready to believe she and Zack could be a couple, but once again putting her trust in Zack had led to something positive. For a short time, she could pretend to just be an aunt. Until this moment, she hadn't realized how much she'd missed the simple act of playing with her niece.

Zack paced the length of the visitors' room of Wyndom Prison. A line of ten chairs sat in front of desks and plexiglass windows. On the other side were matching chairs. Each side had a phone. Prisoners and visitors occupied four sets of seats. Two of the visitors looked well over his age, one looked sick and the other fought to hold both a baby and the phone. The stench of sweat and dust cleaner clogged his nostrils.

It had taken him close to an hour driving the speed limit to get here and most of the time he wished he could've called Parker or Kyle to take on this task. Or even Jessa. But Zack needed to do this himself. He'd know better which questions to ask. Besides, he'd already asked his siblings for too much. They needed to focus on the actual business of bounty hunting.

The barred door behind the prisoners' side opened. A tall, thin man wearing orange overalls shuffled into the room. The man had a full beard, but it couldn't hide the gaunt look on his face. Teddy Copeland.

Zack slid into the plastic chair and picked up the corded phone to his left. The guard who'd escorted Copeland into the room stepped away. With his back to the bars, he crossed his arms and stared straight in front of him.

For a few minutes, Copeland sat watching Zack, as though trying to place him from somewhere. Once he picked up the phone, he shifted his body to one side. "I've been in here almost a year, Mr. Bounty Hunter. I don't know any people who skipped bail and I don't know where they could be. Thanks for stopping by." He pulled the phone from his ear.

Zack wracked his brain for something to keep the man on the phone. "Sheriff Drew Timmins."

Copeland stilled. His gaze of steel drilled into Zack. The man returned the phone to his ear. "I'm listening."

"It was his deputy who arrested you, right?"

"Yeah."

Down the row of visitors, the baby shrieked. "He claimed you had a big stash of crystal meth in your possession, all ready to be sold."

Copeland inched forward. Behind him, an overweight prisoner swaggered toward another guard close to the barred doorway. "I admitted to having the drug in the car but no way did I have as much as they said I did."

"How much did you have?"

"I bought enough for me. I was always careful, you know? I never bought so much that I could be charged with intent to sell. Never. I didn't never push meth on anybody else."

"Yet, that's what you were arrested for."

Copeland glanced to the left, then to the right. "It was the cops, man." He moved even closer to the window and whispered, "They didn't like what I had to say so they framed me."

"Did you tell all this to your lawyer?"

"Yeah, but he couldn't do nothing. Nobody listened. Except for my lawyer, nobody believed me over a decorated deputy and sheriff."

"I do."

The man narrowed his gaze. "What're you saying?"

"I want you to tell me your version of what happened the night you were arrested."

"Are you gonna get me outta here?"

"I can't answer that." Zack shook his head.

Shifting in his seat, Copeland made a *psssht* sound. "Then why should I talk to you?"

"Because the same people who messed with you are messing with a couple of people who mean a lot to me. If I can help bring the true criminals down, then I'll go to bat for you, too."

"Why would you do that? We don't know each other."

"No, but you deserve respect and justice, and I always fight for those."

Copeland stared at Zack, as though too afraid to put any faith in his words. "I got pulled over for a broken taillight. The sheriff ordered me out of the car and searched it. The deputy he rode with found my meth. The deputy walked back to their car. Sheriff asked if I wanted to stay out of jail and keep this off my record."

"Of course you said yes." Zack shrugged.

"Right? Anyways, I said yes, thinking I'd have to be like a snitch or something. But those dudes wanted me to sell drugs to kids and adults, run errands, beat down on people. I'd report to them and I'd get paid, sometimes in drugs, sometimes in cash."

"Then what happened?" he encouraged.

"I told 'em I didn't think it was a good fit for me. I know I have a drug problem, but I ain't a dealer or some-body's muscle. Plus, I thought they might be trying to get me in even more trouble, you know?"

"Yeah, sounded like it."

"Next thing I know, I'm slammed down on the trunk of the car. The deputy held a brown paper bag up by my head."

"Filled with meth?"

"Yes. He told the sheriff he found it under my passenger seat. They took me in, threw me behind bars to face a sentence twice as long as I shoulda faced."

"And you told your lawyer the whole story?"

"Every word. Mr. Capper tried to argue it with the judge, but the judge said it had too many holes in it."

"Have you had any contact with Timmins or any of his guys since?"

Copeland shook his head. "Nope." He tapped his thumb on the handset and stared toward the table. "I tried, too."

Zack frowned. "What do you mean?"

"I told my lawyer I wanted to talk to Timmins. I was

going to tell him I changed my mind and I'd do whatever he wanted. I needed to be free. I wanted to be around to sce my baby girl be born." Tears gathered in the man's eyes. "But he never came. I've been in here since. My little girl doesn't know her daddy."

"I'm sorry, Copeland. I promise I'll do whatever I can for you."

"Really?"

"I can't promise things will get better, but I will try." Zack glanced at the ancient clock hanging over the doorway to the lobby. He'd been here half an hour too long. At least Wyndom was out of Timmins's jurisdiction.

"Thank you."

"I'll keep you in my prayers and I'll get back to you when I can. Thank you for talking with me."

Copeland held up his hand. "Hey, it's not like I had anything better to do." He hung up the phone, stood, then spoke to the guard who'd escorted him in.

Zack's ears buzzed with the conversations continuing around him, but his mind swirled with all the thoughts Copeland's story had generated. He shot another look at the clock before he walked through the door to the exit hallway. This trip had turned out to be a gold mine of information. He thanked the woman behind the counter in the lobby and hurried out the sliding glass doors. The warm, muggy air blasted against him and sweat beaded on his forehead before he reached Greta's vehicle. But he was free. And, God willing, Jamie would soon be, too.

Once he pulled his phone from his pocket, he called Jessa's number. "What's up, my friend?" Most of the time she was a fun-loving woman, but all three of the guys knew to get out of her way when she was in a bad mood.

"Hey, Jessa. I've got another job for you, if you're willing."

"Of course. What do you need?"

"Find out what you can on Teddy Copeland. He's in Wyndom Prison now and he's been arrested before. He's given me some information, but I want to see how much of it I can believe. If you can, visit Copeland's girlfriend."

"Got it. Hey, Kyle and Parker are still investigating the names you gave Kyle last night, but they did find out something about Dan Butler, the guy in charge of the Don't Do Drugs program throughout the state. He was the principal financial backer for Sheriff Timmins's re-election campaign."

"Anything else?"

"I've been looking into the warehouse you and Jamie found the drugs in. I'm not positive yet, but I think I might have a connection between Butler and the property. I haven't gotten very far, though, because we're taking everything slow so Timmins doesn't find out we're investigating him."

"Good thinking." He'd made the choice to assist Jamie and he'd accept his consequences. He didn't want anyone else suffering for his decisions. "Thanks, Jessa."

"Of course. I'll let you know what I find out from the girlfriend, and you keep us posted on your progress, too."

Once they said their goodbyes, Zack hopped into Greta's car, tossed his phone in the console and headed out of the prison parking lot. By the time he returned to the apartment, dark clouds had overtaken the sky. He slid the vehicle into the carport and made his way to Greta's apartment. Silence greeted him along with the scents of an Italian meal cooking in the oven when he stepped into the kitchen. "Jamie?"

No response. No sound at all.

Odd, with a little kid around, unless Charlotte was taking a nap. But what about Greta and Jamie? He set the keys on the counter where he'd picked them up several hours earlier. Pieces of a popular kids' cereal were spread out across the kitchen table. A juice box sat on its side next to a plate with sliced apple pieces already turning brown.

Nothing about the room screamed trouble. But the silence unnerved him. He took a few steps toward the window. The air conditioner kicked in, rustling a few sheets of paper on the edge of the counter. Rain dripped lazily on the bushes outside the window. Zack slowly moved farther into the home. Where was everybody?

He stepped toward the living room. When he reached the archway, he relaxed his shoulders and smiled.

Jamie sat in the rocking chair, sound asleep with the kid at her feet. Charlotte still held on to the tattered elephant. One of its ears had been sewn back on, maybe more than once. With a sweet smile from ear to ear, she looked to be having a conversation with the toy.

Zack seriously considered taking a picture so he could always remember the two of them exactly like this when Jamie went back to her real life and left his. Maybe someday he'd feel competent enough to have a family of his own and a successful career.

Then again, maybe not.

Charlotte turned toward him and waved.

He returned the wave, then pressed his finger to his lips. She imitated his movement, as though directing the stuffed toy. When she looked at Zack again, he motioned her toward him. While she tiptoed over to him, he crouched down.

"I'm glad you're home, Mr. Zack," she whispered.

"Me, too." He playfully tapped the tip of her nose. "How come you're not sleeping?"

The pigtails flopped when she shook her head. "I don't like naps."

"Me, neither. Where's Greta?"

"She went to her room when I first pretended to be asleep. Want to come play with me?"

"Uh."

"Please." She clasped her hands together and tilted her head to one side. The sweet smile added to her charm and Charlotte was one hard-to-resist kid.

Hanging out with a six-year-old in a playroom should be interesting. Zack held his hand out. "Lead the way."

When she slid those tiny fingers into his hand, some of his worries disappeared. She trusted him, quicker than her aunt had, with the innocence only a child could possess. Her eyes held an overload of hope, but still a hint of hesitation.

She urged him down the hall into her pseudo-playroom. "I'm going to color," she said at normal voice level. "You want to, too?" She released his hand, grabbed two coloring books from one of the shelves and skipped over to her kiddie table. A small adult desk sat in the corner of the room with a box of office supplies tucked underneath. Two potted plants sat on the windowsill.

Once Charlotte set the elephant on the table, she grabbed the box of crayons and turned to him. With a smile, she held out a crayon. "You can choose which book you want to color in."

"Okay." He'd seen his sister with little kids. He could do this. He moved to Charlotte's side. Of course, he towered over her, and that bit of hope she held on to stared up at him again. He shoved the little kid plastic chair to one side and sat on the floor.

They colored silently for a few minutes. Maybe while he and Jamie were out tomorrow they could pick up a new elephant. Stuffing stuck out of the trunk and one of the legs. Talk about needing life support.

"It's okay you're not staying in the lines," she said. "You just need to practice."

"Yeah?" His smile widened. She was kind of cute.

She nodded. "My auntie says the more you practice the better you get at stuff."

"She's a smart lady."

"And a really good colorer, too." While she worked, she stuck her tongue out to the side of her mouth.

"Thanks for letting me play with you."

"You're welcome, Mr. Zack."

"Hey." He nudged her shoulder. "Now that we're hanging out together, can you do something for me?"

"Uh-huh." She nodded.

"Can you just call me Zack? You don't have to say mister. It would be like me saying Miss Charlotte every time I talk to you." She laughed. "Or like me calling you Miss Giggly." When he reached forward to tickle her, she laughed louder.

The sound unlatched something within him, something he couldn't quite put his finger on. Memories of his own childhood—of the pranks he and his siblings pulled, of the happy, carefree times with their parents—rushed to the front of his mind. He'd never doubted he was loved.

Did Charlotte?

Did Jamie?

As the moments with the little one passed, Zack felt a duty settle on his heart: to make sure both Charlotte and

Jamie knew they were treasured. How he'd go about letting them know, Zack had no idea, but he'd find a way. He just couldn't do it himself.

Of course he cared for them. He found peace when he spent time with them. Yes, he wanted to see them embrace all life had to offer without fear. But love was still a risk and he wasn't sure he could take the chance. Not even for Jamie and Charlotte.

# EIGHT

Jamie stood in the doorway with her arms crossed and a smile spreading across her mouth. To see her niece interacting so well with Zack warmed her heart. Drew had hardly ever wanted to be around Charlotte and often claimed work took him away. Jamie had also worried how Erin's abuse would affect her niece, but children were resilient in ways no adult could understand.

When Jamie first saw him in the internet café, Zack looked tough, determined. Now, he sat with her niece, decorating a picture of a kitten and chatting about princesses. "Not so tough after all," she whispered, then spoke up. "I see Charlotte's made a new friend."

"Yes, she has." Zack rested his hand over his knee and smiled up to her.

"I'm helping Mr. Zack color in the lines."

He leaned closer to Charlotte. "You're helping who?"

With an exaggerated sigh, she answered, "Zack."

He motioned between her niece and himself. "We're close enough now we're on a first-name basis."

"I see." Jamie lowered her arms. "Well, why don't we let him get back to his own work? We can help Greta get supper ready."

"No, Auntie. Please let him stay to finish his picture."

"Charlotte," Jamie warned.

"We're good." Zack winked at her niece. "The two of us can wait together until dinner's ready. Besides, I do want to finish my coloring."

"Are you sure?" Jamie chuckled.

He shrugged. "Yeah. I'll fill you in on my good road trip after dinner."

"All right, then. We'll call you when the food's ready." She turned and walked to the kitchen.

Greta had already started picking up the random pieces of cereal dropped on the table. "The stuffed shells are almost done."

Jamie grabbed silverware from the drawer by the oven. "Good. I'm hungry."

As she wiped off and set the table, her niece's laughter drifted down the hallway. Again, she smiled. "Charlotte's teaching Zack how to color in the lines."

"Sounds like they're having fun." Greta grabbed plates out of the dishwasher.

"With all Charlotte's been through, I was a little worried about introducing them." She began setting the table. "But he's turning out to be a good influence."

"For both Charlotte and you." Greta bumped her shoulder.

"Don't start, Greta."

Her friend walked to the oven. "Okay, but consider one more thing and then I'll leave you alone." No, she wouldn't. Jamie rolled her eyes. Greta was like a puppy with a new toy. She didn't know when to let go.

"Yes?" Jamie waited until her friend served the cheesy pasta, then took two of the plates to the table.

Greta set the other two down on the place mats. "What if you're exactly what he needs, too?" She gave Jamie's elbow a gentle squeeze as she slid by and wandered down the hall.

Could she be? There was no denying she enjoyed the times with him when they spoke of real life instead of Drew. Plus, she loved laughing with him and learning whatever she could about him. And she couldn't forget the kiss. She wrapped her arms around herself and brought back the memory of how his mouth felt covering hers, how much comfort and adventure she tasted in his lips.

So many wishes and hopes, some from when she was a little girl, rushed through her head. As she'd thought before, Zack Owen might be her protector, her partner, but she wanted him for so much more.

"Crazy thoughts," she whispered.

But were they? Zack had become a special part of her life in such a short time, and their connection intensified each day. Was Zack's presence in her life to let her know God had finally forgiven her for not being there for Erin? Did He deem her worthy of His blessing again now that she fought to protect Charlotte and bring Drew down?

Her niece's laughter rushed down the hallway along with Greta and Zack's conversation.

After a stop in the bathroom to wash their hands, her niece guided Zack to a chair at the table. Once everyone was seated, Charlotte asked, "Greta, can I say grace?"

"Sure can, kiddo."

Her niece prayed? Jamie glanced at Greta, who shrugged sheepishly. "We've been worried about you."

Charlotte grabbed Jamie's hand and then Zack's. Greta joined in the hand-holding. "Dear God, thank You for bringing my auntie back even if it's just for a little while.

Thank You, too, for Zack, who's doing a great job helping Auntie Jamie."

As Charlotte continued her prayer, Jamie peeked over her niece's head at Zack. He winked at her and his smile broadened. They sat there, quiet, together, strengthening a bond she'd never expected to share.

Was she good enough?

"And don't forget my daddy. He needs Your love more than any of us. Okay, that's all for now. Amen."

"Sweetie, you pray for your father?" Jamie would pray he got shot during a fight with a criminal, or he ran into traffic when he chased a fugitive.

"Uh-huh." Charlotte brushed her bangs from her forehead. "Even though he's mean sometimes, he still deserves God's love."

Silence engulfed the room as all the adults stilled. The man had ruined part of Charlotte's life, yet she remained positive about him. Tears stung the corners of Jamie's eyes as she leaned down and kissed her niece on the cheek. "You are such a special little girl."

"I know." She sat up straight and grinned.

"Let's eat!" Zack slapped his hands together before diving into his meal.

Once they'd finished supper, Charlotte helped Greta clean up while Zack sat with Jamie on the living room couch. The excited chatter of the six-year-old blended in with the sound of the flowing water and the clanking of dishes. Jamie grabbed a pen and the journal from her backpack.

"Okay, what can you tell me?" Jamie's determined, all-business, fugitive expression replaced the playful, carefree aunt one.

To be truthful, Zack mourned the loss.

"Zack?" Jamie waved her hand in front of his face. "You with me?"

"Yeah." He shifted forward and draped his forearms over his thighs. "Copeland was a great help. He claims the amount of crystal meth he was arrested for having was way more than he actually had."

"Which means someone's lying."

Zack nodded slowly. "He was quick to add the arresting lawmen gave him a choice. He could basically become their gopher, doing whatever they needed whenever they needed it."

"Or?"

"Go to jail."

She tapped the pen against the cover of the journal. "Who arrested him?"

"Want to take a guess?" From the tightness in her jaw, he was pretty sure she already knew.

Jamie tossed up both hands. "Drew and George?"

"Bingo. Copeland went on to say when he refused the side job, Linden planted a lot more of the drug and set the wheels in motion for Copeland to be sent to prison for possession with intent to sell. Once I—"

Jamie held her palm up. "Hold on."

Zack remained quiet while Jamie jotted notes on a new page of the journal. "Okay, continue," she directed.

"Once I left the prison, I started thinking about how we could get this corroborated. So I called Jessa to get one of my partners to look into Copeland. In the meantime, Parker went to interview the family of a different guy on the list your sister left you. He called me back as soon as he left the apartment. He asked point-blank how much of a drug addict the man had been. The widow said she was surprised when the deputies stated how little meth was in his car. She said he'd been an addict most of his life and she knew the amount of meth the deputy claimed he had wouldn't have done much for him."

"Who arrested him?"

"Linden. The guy was released and, get this, Timmins became like a mentor to him until the day he died...of a drug overdose."

Jamie tapped the pen on her lips as she thought. The air conditioner kicked on. "So drugs were placed in Beth's car, all ten men on Erin's list were either arrested for drug possession or are involved in drug-free programs." She drew little boxes on the edge of the journal page.

"Don't forget the warehouse." Where he'd been helpless to stop Timmins from hurting her.

*Let it go.*

"Right." She brushed her bangs out of her eyes. Just like Charlotte did. With a hint of a smile, Zack glanced toward the kitchen, where the little girl continued talking. Poor Greta must be exhausted.

Jamie covered her face with her hands as a yawn passed through her. "I wish I could find something besides circumstantial evidence to connect Drew to all of this illegal activity. Then we'd have enough to go straight to the state police."

"Let's look at the pictures again. We have a lot more information." While she searched her backpack, he shifted Greta's Bible and one of Charlotte's dolls to the side of the coffee table. "Maybe something else will jump out at us."

She handed half the pile of photographs to him. "Some of my personal pictures might be mixed in with Erin and

Beth's since we've had everything in my backpack. Just put them on the side." As she sifted through her own handful, she set some in a pile and the rest she laid out one by one on the table.

The faucet in the kitchen turned off. Although he couldn't make out Greta's words, he could hear her speaking to Charlotte.

Most of the photos were of Jamie's brother-in-law with various men, some who looked familiar and some he'd never seen before. Zack stilled when he came to the next photo. Jamie and Charlotte had on fancy, flowery dresses. Waves crashed behind them. The wind lifted Jamie's hair, which was several inches longer than it was now. She kept hold of her niece's hand and they both had wide, carefree smiles. To say she looked beautiful would be an understatement. "Wow."

"What?" She inched closer, her thigh bumping his. "Did you find an incriminating one?" She leaned over and tugged on the picture. "Oh, I forgot I had this one. We were down on Blue Shutters Beach. It was Mother's Day two years ago. I took Erin and Charlotte out for lunch."

He almost thought to tuck the photograph away in his pocket when she wasn't looking. Going back to business, Jamie set several other personal pictures in the pile on the table. "Do you think it was Beth or your sister who took all the pictures in their investigation?"

"Beth, for sure. Erin wouldn't have had the courage to spy this closely on Drew." Sadness covered her face. "I never knew my sister had relied on Beth for so much." Her hand shook as she brushed her fingertips across another photo with Charlotte and Erin. "Maybe I could've…" Tears dripped down Jamie's cheeks.

Zack wrapped his arm around her shoulders. "You did

what you could for her and you're protecting her daughter. No one can ask for more."

"If I had answered the call instead of sitting there laughing and joking with my friends, she could still be alive."

A lightbulb went on his head. So guilt was the cause of her fierce determination. Now he understood. But the guilt had no right to rip her apart from inside. He cupped her chin and brushed another set of tears away. "Jamie, you are not responsible for your sister's death. Timmins is."

"But I turned my back on her." She sniffled and dropped a few more tears.

The crying cut into his heart. "No, you didn't. You took a vacation with friends. Erin wouldn't want you to blame yourself." He pressed his mouth to hers and tasted the salty mixture of her tears. "You need to find a way to forgive yourself."

"I don't know, Zack." She shook her head.

"Jamie, you're beautiful, you're kindhearted, you're selfless and you deserve your own happiness as much as anyone else." He bent his head and covered her mouth with his own. The tenderness of her lips ignited his insides and opened one of the last chinks of chain link he'd wrapped around his heart. Time stood still. Her fingers drifted down his neck and settled on his chest. He caressed the back of her head. Yes, they'd kissed before, but this one was different. Longer, more intense, desperate, a shift in their relationship. Hopefully as much for her as for him.

Out of the corner of his eye, he saw movement. Greta cleared her throat. "Guys."

As though guilty of wrongdoing, Jamie pulled out of

his hold and swiped her fingers over her face. Zack didn't care if Greta caught him kissing Jamie. She needed solace and he wanted to be there for her.

Okay, maybe he hadn't needed to kiss her. Twice.

Greta smiled. Yep, the woman had witnessed at least the end of the kiss. "Charlotte's getting a drink, then she'll be in here with you. I'll be back in a few minutes."

"Got it." As her cheeks grew red, Jamie kept her gaze glued to the coffee table.

While Greta walked down the hall, Charlotte skipped into the living room with a juice box in one hand and the ever-faithful elephant in the other. "Whatcha doing?"

"Looking at pictures," Zack explained as the little one snuggled in between him and Jamie. The scent of generic kiddie shampoo drifted up to his nose.

She glanced at the next picture Jamie set down, one of Hampton Waterfront Complex. "Ooh!" Charlotte's eyes grew wide as saucers. The biggest smile he'd seen on her took over her face. "Can we go back there? It was fun."

Jamie frowned. "In here?" She pointed to the warehouse she and Zack had broken into. In this picture, Timmins and another man stood by the door.

"No, silly. We went to the park across the water. I remember 'cause the scary ride is right there." She pointed to the roller-coaster tracks in the right corner of the photo. "Daddy didn't make me go on the scary rides." Suddenly her mouth curved into an O. Uneasiness crept into her face. "Uh-oh."

"What's wrong, sweet pea?" Zack asked.

She sucked on the straw of her juice box. "I'm not supposed to tell."

Jamie and Zack locked gazes. "If he hurt her…" she said barely above a whisper.

Zack held up his hand, then shifted so his face was in front of Charlotte. "Sweet pea, your dad has made a lot of bad choices. Telling you to keep secrets is one of them. Your aunt and I need you to be honest more today than any other day so far in your life."

She refused to look at him. Her grip on the elephant tightened.

Zack tucked a finger under her chin and made her meet his gaze. "Charlotte, what would your mom say?"

"Mommy would say listen to you because you're friends with my auntie, who knows everything."

"Well, maybe not everything." Zack smiled as he looked over the kid's head to catch Jamie's reaction.

She pursed her lips but couldn't hold the look. She, too, grinned. "Go on, Charlotte."

"Daddy took me to the park one day. But we had to stop at that building first. I stayed in the car. Daddy and Mr. George took something out of the trunk. It was big because they're really strong and it took both of them to lift."

Jamie took the little girl's hands in her own. "Did you see what it was?"

"No." Her pigtails bounced with the shake of her head.

"What did they do with it?" He kept his voice casual.

"Daddy had told me not to move from my seat, but I turned around and saw they put it on the ground on this side of this building." She pointed to the same area he and Jamie had parked in. "Then there was a big splash in the water. Mr. George got mad and yelled at Daddy, then Daddy came back in the car. He made me promise not to tell we came here. It was scary. His eyes got really little and his voice sounded mean. I promised. Then he took me to the park."

A secret stop. Linden arguing with Timmins. A big, heavy item they lifted from the trunk and dumped in Narragansett Bay. He sat up straight. "Do you think we've figured out what happened to Beth?"

"I need to go back to the waterfront." Jamie hastily gathered the pictures she'd spread out between them on the table.

"No, we don't. *We* need to let the state police handle everything from here on out."

She stopped cold with the pictures clenched in her hands. "This could be the nail in the coffin for Drew."

Charlotte scratched her head. "Aren't coffins for dead people?"

"Yes, sweet pea."

"If we're right, this is proof he's not fit to be a parent, let alone the sheriff. I need to find the evidence." When she spoke, she almost spit nails. Once she opened her backpack, she shoved the pictures inside.

"How do you expect to find it? Are you planning to jump in the bay and swim down to find what the men dropped in the water?"

"I don't know. We could search for any other clues around the premises to prove Drew's involvement with the crates. We could see if anyone from the neighboring businesses has anything to say, maybe about what they might've seen."

"It's nighttime. They're closed."

"You don't know that for sure."

"Jamie…" In this discussion, it wasn't hard for him to remain professional. His direction was based on common sense, which she had clearly lost.

"Then we could investigate ourselves, see if Drew or any of his men are there tonight getting busy with their second job." As though she'd decided her next move, she nodded.

Tension simmered between them. Why was she being difficult all of a sudden? Was she overwhelmed? Feeling the overload of guilt? He tried to keep his voice calm. "Let the police handle it."

Her eyes narrowed as she stood.

He stood up next to her. "Do you remember what happened the first time we went? Don't be reckless." Wasn't it his job to keep her from doing something she'd regret? He had to keep her safe. "You won't be able to do anything until tomorrow."

"Then what about your family? Will they go down there?"

"Tonight? No." Good grief. "What's happened to your brain?"

Charlotte stepped back. Greta appeared at the hallway entrance. She remained quiet. Worry filled her and the kid's expressions.

Jamie pressed her palm over her heart. "I'm going down there." Her voice grew louder.

When she turned to leave the room, he grabbed her wrist. "No, you're not."

"Let go of me." She pulled her hand, but he tightened his hold.

"Nothing's going to change through the night. Tomorrow morning is soon enough."

"Zack." She tugged her wrist harder. "Remove your hand. You're hurting me."

"No." But he did loosen his hold immediately.

Charlotte barged forward and pounded her tiny fists against Zack's thigh and arm. "Let Auntie Jamie go!"

Her pigtails did their own kind of dance. "Don't you be mean to her!"

*What in the world?* Zack released Jamie. Raising his arms, he stared down at the pint-size person.

Jamie pulled her niece away from him and wrapped her arms around the kid. "It's okay, sweetie. I'm all right."

Of course. The kid had been traumatized by watching her father argue with and abuse her mother for years. Zack should've remembered that. But they knew he'd never hurt Jamie. Right? "Yeah, you're okay. It's me. Now let your niece go and sit back down so I can finish telling you why you're wrong." He reached forward.

Jamie shifted back. "You aren't going to tell me anything. Don't touch me."

*God, take away my aggravation and give me strength to be patient here.*

Charlotte tore herself from Jamie's arms. One elephant ear hung crooked as she ran from the room, crying all the way.

He walked toward the hallway, then stopped. Should he go talk to Charlotte or stay to reason with Jamie? Something tightened in his chest.

"I'll go talk to her." Jamie took a step toward him, but Greta stood in her way.

"No, I'll go," Zack said, but he still didn't move. Which choice meant more?

"She needs me, not you." Jamie's words stuck in him like a craw.

"I have to make things right with her." Zack walked toward the bedrooms. Greta's words shifted to mumbles as Charlotte's sniffles got louder. He stood in the doorway of her room with his hands on his hips. The kid had squished herself between the bed and the nightstand, then pulled her knees to her chest with the elephant stuffed in between.

What was he supposed to do now? He didn't know how best to stop the little one from crying. What if his attempt made her cry even harder? Yes, he'd been able to keep Jamie and Charlotte happy with his efforts to protect them, but them both losing faith in him tossed him into uncharted territory. Should he make Charlotte laugh or should he talk seriously to her? And would it still be possible for her to like him?

This was exactly why he had no business allowing his feelings to get mixed in with his duty.

But he had to do something right now.

"Charlotte?" He slipped inside the room.

"I'm sorry. I won't hit you again." Panic flooded her face with each step closer he took. "I'll be good. I promise."

A sickening feeling lodged in the center of his chest. The reality of what had been happening in the Timmins house slugged into his gut. He clenched his jaw, closed his fists.

Charlotte's eyes widened, then clamped shut. "I said I was sorry. I really am." Tears sprang loose again and dripped down her cheeks.

As he crouched down in front of her, he forced a deep breath through his system. He raised his hand, but should he touch her? Or would the feel of his fingers only scare her more? "Sweet pea, open your eyes for me." He kept his hands to himself for the time being. When she did as he asked, she hiccupped. "Did your daddy ever hit you when you did something wrong?"

She wrapped herself tighter. "Only once, but he'd say stuff and yell and hit my mom a lot."

Zack fought the rage growing stronger inside him. But he had to let it go. God would judge Timmins. Zack's job was to stand up for the law. To reach that goal, tonight's assignment entailed making sure the girls, both Jamie and Charlotte, felt safe.

Yes, they were an *assignment*. Not friends, not family, nothing more than two people he needed to assist.

He moved his hand. Charlotte's eyes followed its path. More tears streamed down her cheeks. As he placed his palms on each of her knees, a set of whimpers escaped her mouth. "Can I tell you something?" he asked.

She nodded.

"I might get mad at your aunt or maybe even you, but I promise I will never hurt either of you."

She hiccupped again. "Never ever?"

He shook his head. "Never ever."

"Pinkie promise?" She whispered as she released the hold she had on her legs.

He leaned closer to her, latched his little finger to hers and smiled. "Absolutely." Slowly he brushed his thumb across her cheek to wipe away her tears. Should he pick her up? Hug her? Not touch her at all?

Too many choices and no guarantee which one was the best.

Once he'd moved back enough for her to get up without feeling intimidated, he held out his hand. "Come on. Let's go check on your aunt."

She crawled out to him, slid her hand in his and they both got to their feet. She glanced up at him with a tiny bit of hope.

Earlier he'd thought about how great they all were together, how fulfilling it might be to have a family. Clearly, he'd been delusional. Tomorrow they'd go their separate ways. He'd toss all feelings aside and go back to focusing on his bounty hunting duties.

When they took steps from the middle of the room, something dropped from the elephant. Charlotte looked to the carpet. "Whoa." She crouched down and picked the item up. "Why would my elephant throw up Mommy's cell phone?"

Zack's nerves tightened as he reached out for it. Bingo. "I think I know what this is. Something from your mom to help us—" *nail your father* "—prove how scary your dad is." He joined Charlotte in studying the hole in the elephant's ear and the ripped stiches in it. "Come on. We need to show your auntie."

As she and Greta stood by the kitchen, Jamie rubbed her arms. "Yes, you're right, Greta. I should've tried to stay calm before I said anything to Zack."

"Aren't I always right?" Her friend grinned.

"Most of the time." Jamie smiled until Zack walked down the hallway with a hard determination in his expression. Guilt crushed her insides even as the intensity of his gaze forced her back a few steps.

Greta pressed her palm on Jamie's back and whispered, "Go on."

"Zack, I'm sorry." He'd been nothing but good to her and she'd made him angry by arguing with him because he didn't agree with her. "I shouldn't have—"

"Later." He held up the phone. "We have work to do."

Greta gasped behind her. Jamie's jaw dropped. "Where did that come from?"

"My elephant." Charlotte stood up straight and smiled. "Mommy left us a surprise."

"Yes, she did." Jamie turned to Greta. "Can you…?"

She tilted her head toward Charlotte and then to the living room.

Greta nodded. "Come on, kiddo. Let's watch TV for a bit." As Greta and Charlotte moved toward the couch, with Greta promising to sew the elephant's ear back on later, Jamie followed Zack down the hall.

"Let's hope there's incriminating evidence on here." He turned the phone on. Of course it had a security screen. "Do you know what your sister's code is?"

When they entered Charlotte's temporary room, she followed Zack to the bed and sat beside him, close enough to smell a hint of his unique scent. "No. That's not Erin's phone. Drew wouldn't let her have one like this. He gave her a flip phone with no internet access just so she could make calls if she needed. It's got to be Beth's, and I have no idea what her code would be." They couldn't come this close to solving the case and not find answers.

Zack shrugged. "Or Beth got it for your sister. When she saw it, Charlotte called it 'Mommy's cell phone.' What's something Erin would use for a password, something you'd easily figure out?"

"Charlotte's birthday would be the most logical. October 11."

Zack punched in one, zero, one, one. The screen opened up like a gate. "Here we go."

"Let's see the pictures." Jamie set her hand on his arm, his skin feeling warm against her fingertips.

Zack scrolled through the photos, but none had to do with Drew or his illegal activities. "Nothing." He continued going through the photo app and stopped at a picture of her brother-in-law in a video.

Energy stirred within her. "Wait. Is that Drew in the video?"

"Yep." Zack pressed the Play button. Drew and George sat in the backyard with Charlotte giggling as she ran around in the background.

*"I thought when we got rid of my housekeeper, everything would go back to normal."*

*"Why? What's happening?"*

*"Erin's different, bolder. She's still asking too many questions and sticking her nose where it doesn't belong."*

*"Daddy, come play with me on the swings."* Charlotte ran over to the men and slid her hand into her father's. The person taking the video sank closer to the ground.

Drew yanked his arm away. *"Didn't I tell you not to bother me when I'm working?"*

Charlotte's smile disappeared. In its place was…fear. *"I'm sorry, Daddy."* With her thumb in her mouth, she backed several feet away before she turned and ran.

Jamie's throat tightened.

*"My wife is becoming too much of a liability for us, especially with Beth dead."*

*"We could plant the crystal meth on her, too. Then people will assume she and your housekeeper were doing drugs together,"* George offered.

*"Good idea. That way, if Erin becomes too much of a problem, then I'll have a plan in motion to get rid of her, too."*

George nodded.

The person holding the phone, presumably Erin, gasped and juggled the screen. When Drew glanced her way, she shoved herself even closer to the ground.

Tears gathered in the corners of Jamie's eyes.

Seconds ticked by until Drew looked away from her

sister's direction. Pavement whooshed with plant stems across the screen. Then the video ended.

"So, it couldn't have been Beth who took the video," Zack said. "She was already dead at this point."

Moisture threatened to fall from Jamie's eyes, so she blew out a breath. "The video was taken the day Drew killed Erin. Charlotte was wearing the same dress and she had the same barrette in her hair when I arrived later. Erin must've known she'd never get away so she sewed the phone in the elephant hoping someone besides Drew would find it."

"You know what this means, right?"

"Yeah." She clasped her hands together then dropped them to her lap. "With the information we and your family have found and the video, we have enough proof to put Drew, and George for that matter, behind bars for years."

"Exactly." He nodded. "Plus, this will support your case for taking Charlotte. You won't be cleared of kidnapping her or of the assault on Timmins because you kind of did do those things, but hopefully the courts will see you were justified."

"Good, because I'm all Charlotte has left."

"And it sounds like the police will find Beth's body weighted down deep in Narragansett Bay."

"All this time, all our efforts are finally going to pay off."

"See?" He held out his hands. "You just need a little faith."

"I have to admit, God has come through. It may not have been the way I wanted everything to happen, but He did take care of us."

"He has His own plan, but He'll always be there for you."

"As you have been. I'm sorry, Zack, for the way I reacted to you earlier. You were right to make me think first."

"I'm sorry, too. After everything you and Charlotte have been through, I should've handled the situation differently."

"You've been nothing but kind and considerate from the day I met you. You've played with my niece and supported me."

"I'm just a man who wants to see justice done. Don't make me out to be a hero."

"But you are to me. I don't think I would've survived these past few days without you." Thankfully she'd never have to find out. So much hope swirled through her and her heart warmed. "I'm thankful I have you in my life." She reached for his hand, inched closer to him and pressed her mouth to his.

Yes, things would change when they got back to Rhode Island, but she didn't need to think about that yet. For the moment, he was still beside her, still within her reach, still a bright light pulling her out of the darkness she'd forced herself in. For now, she would enjoy every moment she could.

But the light died quickly.

Zack tugged his hand free and gently pushed her back. "Jamie, I don't think this is a good idea."

Heat surged up her neck and flooded her cheeks. He kept his gaze on her, but she couldn't meet it. "I'm sorry. I didn't mean to…" She pressed her lips together and tucked her hair behind her ear. Didn't mean to throw herself at him?

"It's just that tomorrow things change."

"Of course." She nodded. "You'll go back to chasing real criminals and I'll get busy raising Charlotte."

"You're a wonderful woman with a good heart."

Just not the woman for him. She got it. They had different dreams, different roles in God's plan.

"You'll find someone who—"

"Please don't." She already felt foolish. Zack trying to placate her only made it worse. Standing, she brushed moisture from under her eyes. "I'll leave the phone with you." Yes, focus on the job at hand. Erase anything personal from their interactions. She rushed toward the doorway.

"Jamie, wait."

But she kept walking. What was the point of stopping?

The well-known song of a kids show flew through the hallway. Charlotte began singing off-key as Jamie slid into the bathroom and shut the door. The tears fell freely as she sat on the edge of the tub and pressed her hand over her mouth. She'd been humiliated enough. Allowing him or Greta to hear her crying would mortify her.

Zack had made her feel comfortable, supported and like she mattered. Spending time with him had allowed her to believe in a happy, satisfying future. And he'd kissed her.

What a fool she'd been to get her hopes up. She'd failed her sister. If Erin couldn't have her happily-ever-after, then why should Jamie? Her life's duty had to rest only on Charlotte and in raising her to be someone Erin could be proud of.

Still, she cried for what she and Zack could've been and she cried for all she'd never hold.

The flow of tears slowed. On the other side of the door, feet blocked the light. Jamie sat up straight. *Don't you knock to check on me.* A few more seconds passed and then the light returned. She released a breath she hadn't known she'd been holding.

Once she stood, she checked herself in the mirror. Red eyes stared back at her. She groaned, then splashed water on her face. She'd be strong. She wouldn't cry again because God had been by her side and even though she'd be alone, He wouldn't abandon her. Right? She had her niece, her health, her brother-in-law going to jail. Despite losing Zack tomorrow, Jamie had so much to be thankful for.

The next morning, Zack insisted on an early start for their trip back to the family business. Once he'd parked, he reached into the back seat of the car and picked Charlotte up. Without a sound, she set her head on his shoulder and pressed her tiny palm against his chest. The familiar scent of…kid seeped into his nostrils. He had to admit he'd miss the automatic trust Charlotte had for him once they went their separate ways.

He'd also miss Jamie. His gaze shifted to the passenger side, where she tossed her backpack over her shoulder and grabbed his duffel bag. After she shut the door and joined him on the sidewalk, he wanted to hold his hand toward her. He already missed the intimacy they'd been sharing. The intimacy he put an end to last night when he gave her the "you're a great lady" speech.

But it was the right decision for all of them. She deserved a romance and he had no plan to provide one.

He kept his hand to himself.

Light came out of the windows of Second Chance Bail Bonds and the front door was unlocked. Yet there was no sign of his sister when they stepped inside. "Lil?"

No answer. Her radio softly played some sappy tune.

"Maybe she's in the bathroom," Jamie offered.

Zack set Charlotte on the couch and covered her little body with the afghan on the arm of the chair nearby. After Jamie placed their bags on the vacant seat, she rubbed her arms and turned to stare outside the window. Zack itched to pull her into his arms. Instead, he planted his hands on his hips. "What are you thinking about?"

"How ready I am for the day to be over." She spoke with tension in her voice. Her words felt like a good slap to his ego. Was she that ready to send him off, too? Yes, he'd been the one to terminate their growing relationship, but he hadn't counted on…still wanting her.

Zack's phone rang, cutting into his thoughts.

Jamie turned to Charlotte, then him. "Don't wake her."

He dug his phone from his pocket and recognized the number. "Hey, Kyle."

"Morning," his brother greeted him. "Logan and I are on the way, but there's a huge backup on 295. I'm not sure when we'll get there."

"No problem. We'll be here when you come in."

"You're already at the office?"

"Yeah, but nobody else is yet." He scanned the lights on in the office. "Well, Lily's somewhere."

"Okay, I'll call you when we get going again."

"Got it." As he disconnected the call, he faced Jamie. "Kyle's on his way with our detective friend, Logan." He glanced at the time on his phone. "I don't have a clue where Lil is."

He punched his sister's number into his phone. It rang in his ear…and in the room. Zack and Jamie stared at each other. Dread surfaced within him. "That's my sister's phone." They followed the sound to the desk. He hung up the call. Lily's handbag sat on its side in her chair with its contents sprawled around the floor. Her keys lay in a puddle of coffee next to a broken mug.

Knots formed in his gut. His sweet, innocent sister had been taken. "Timmins."

For a moment, he froze. What should he do now?

Jamie placed her hand on his arm. "We'll find her. I promise."

"You can't promise something like that." The reality of them finding her safe and unharmed fell apart with every passing second. No, he couldn't think like that.

But his mind refused to stop running in circles. He rubbed his hand over his head. "I've got to call Kyle back." And where was Parker?

Zack's phone rang. A number he didn't recognize flashed on his screen, but he accepted the call. "Hello?"

"Listen to me carefully, Mr. Bounty Hunter. If you ever want to see your sister again, you'll bring Jamie and my daughter to my building on the waterfront."

Zack's insides turned to stone. "How do I know you haven't killed her already?" Silence raised the tension within him.

Timmins mumbled, "Say something to your brother."

"Don't turn them over!" Lily demanded.

A thwack grabbed a yelp from his sister. All Zack wanted was to rip something apart. Or someone.

The crooked sheriff continued, "If you don't do as I say, little Miss Lily will die."

His vision blurred. Blood thumped through him fast enough for him to hear it. "Timmins, don't you dare—"

"You've got one hour." The phone line went dead.

# NINE

Jamie's brother-in-law had stolen Zack's sister. Oh, this was so not good.

"This is my worst nightmare." Zack pressed his palms to his temples. "He wants me to turn you and Charlotte over to get her back."

Jamie's stomach clenched. "You're not giving him Charlotte." She shook her head.

"Of course I'm not," Zack snapped.

She nodded. "But I'll go." Zack's sister had helped them before. Jamie couldn't allow an innocent woman to be sacrificed for her.

"No, you won't."

"Why not?"

"Because I won't let you, that's why." He narrowed his gaze as though she'd offered a stupid option.

"Zack, I can't let your sister suffer for my choices."

"If you go, your brother-in-law will torture you until you give up Charlotte and then he'll kill you. I care about you too much to let that happen."

He *what*?

The heavy metal crunch of the back door rushed down the hall. Zack stepped in front of Jamie.

"Doughnuts for everybody!" a woman's cheery voice announced before she stepped into the room. Jessa. Jamie recognized her from the back of the SUV when she and Zack's brothers picked them up in Champlain Park.

"And hot coffee." Parker stepped to Jessa's side. Their smiles disappeared. "What's wrong?"

"Timmins has Lil."

"Whoa." Jessa placed the bags on the desk.

Parker almost dropped the cardboard containers of coffees. "What?" He set the drinks next to the doughnuts.

*God, please take care of our sister.*

Zack nodded. "He took her from here."

Jamie wrung her hands. "He wants your brother to turn me and my niece over to him."

"Well, you're not going to." Jessa crossed her arms. "We have to come up with something better."

"Well, we better do it fast." Zack scanned the time on his phone. "We have an hour."

"Jamie and Jessa will take care of Charlotte, then Zack and I will handle Timmins and get Lily back," Parker explained.

"No," Jessa said at the same time as Jamie and Zack.

"I'm not going to fight about this." Parker glared at his brother. "Zack, I'm staying with you."

"No, you're not." Zack stuffed his phone in his pocket. "This guy wants Jamie for Lily. She has to go."

"Lil's my sister, too." Parker set his hands on his hips.

"Kyle's bringing Logan. Between them and us, we'll get Lily back safe and sound."

"Kyle and Logan aren't here to back you up." The brothers tried to stare each other down. Time ticked by.

Jamie clasped her fingers together. "Parker, please. I need you with Jessa to make sure my niece is safe. With my sister gone, Charlotte is all I have and the more protection I can get for her, the better."

"Jess can protect Charlotte. You guys need someone to watch your backs."

Zack glanced at her, then back to his brother. "I've got Jamie and she has me."

"I don't like it." Parker shifted, his gaze drifting from her to Zack to Jessa.

Whimpers floated from the other side of the room as Charlotte began to stir. The painful moans of the child nearly broke Jamie's heart. No little one should be forced to deal with so much torment.

"Let me go check on her." And plan how to get them all out of this...disaster.

As Jamie wandered across the room, hushed voices clashed behind her. She sat at the end of the couch. "Shh, baby. You're all right." She brushed Charlotte's hair from her face.

A few seconds passed before Charlotte woke up. Reddened eyes sparkling with tears glanced at Jamie. She tapped her thighs. "Come on." The child scrambled to sit in her lap and latched her hands behind Jamie's neck. So much trust her niece had. And it was automatic, nothing she had to think about. How wonderful it must be to still have that innocence. Jamie had lost that too many years ago.

One could argue she was on her way to giving Zack her complete trust that quickly.

Several seconds later, Zack wandered over and sat beside her. Parker and Jessa remained by the front desk. It sounded like they were still arguing. As if it was the most natural thing in the world, Zack brushed his hand over Charlotte's head then down her back.

Jamie kissed the top of the girl's head. "Do we have a plan yet?"

"We're getting there." He shifted to his signature pose, with each forearm leaning on his knees and his hands clasped. "Parker and Jessa are taking Charlotte out of here. They'll take good care of her and keep her safe until we know the police won't give her back to Timmins."

"Makes sense." She nodded.

"Hey, Charlotte." Zack pushed the girl's hair off her shoulder. "You're going away for a little longer." As he spoke, Jessa walked toward them and Parker pulled out his cell phone.

"Again?"

"Yeah. It's so we can solve the problems with your father so you don't have to be afraid anymore." As he explained their decision to a six-year-old, Jamie ran her fingers through her niece's fine dark hair. "I promise we'll get Auntie Jamie back to you as soon as possible."

Charlotte lifted her pain-filled gaze to Jamie. Her voice was barely above a whisper. "I'm scared."

So was Jamie.

"Sweet pea, I promise you'll be safe. My friend Jessa's going to stay with you until we can all be together again," Zack promised. Parker continued some conversation by the desk.

Jessa waved. "Hi, Charlotte. It's nice to meet you."

"Hi."

"Are you hungry? Because I'm hungry for breakfast. I want some eggs and hash browns."

Charlotte kept her cheek on Jamie's shoulder. "Pancakes?"

"Sure. Then we'll watch some cartoons and before you know it, your aunt will be back." She leaned down. "Plus, I hear you like to color so we'll stop on the way and get you some new crayons and coloring books."

Charlotte perked up, with wide eyes. "Okay."

"Time to go, sweet pea." Zack picked up Jamie's niece and set her on her own two feet.

Jessa held out her hand. "Ready, kiddo?"

Charlotte slid her fingers inside Jessa's but kept her gaze on Jamie. "Auntie Jamie, who's gonna keep you safe?"

"That's my job." Zack playfully tweaked her nose. "Don't worry, sweet pea, I've got it covered."

"We better get going." Jessa pretended to remember something. "Oh, we do have to take one more person with us."

"Who?" Charlotte asked.

As he moved to Jessa's side, Parker kept his hands in his pockets and smiled. "Me." At six foot four, Parker could probably be intimidating to grown men, never mind a six-year-old.

Charlotte glanced over her head. "Whoa." Her tiny lips remained in an O shape. "You're really tall." She inched backward until she bumped into Jamie's legs, the shabby elephant clutched in her hands.

Jessa playfully smacked Parker in the chest. "Yeah, but don't worry about him. He's a big softy."

Zack stood and urged them all to the back door. "You should go."

"I still don't like this plan, but Kyle and Logan agreed with you."

Jessa slapped Parker on the back. "Come on, big guy."

"Wait. There's one more thing." Zack walked to the nearby lounge chair. Once he pulled Beth's cell phone from the backpack, he handed it to his brother. "Here's the proof of Timmins admitting to killing his housekeeper and planning to kill his wife. It's safer in your hands than in the office."

Parker tapped the phone in his palm. "Call me the second you have any news."

"You know it."

After she and Zack hugged Charlotte, Jamie watched Jessa and Parker walk out the back door with her niece, the most important person in her life. "Where are they taking her?" she asked. Zack remained silent beside her. The back door slammed shut with a loud boom. She turned to him. "Zack, where are they going?"

He met her gaze. "I'm not telling you."

"What?" Had she heard him correctly? "What do you mean you're not telling me?"

"We all think it's best you don't know."

She glanced toward the vacant hallway. "No, *we* all don't." As she narrowed her gaze on him, she continued, "I didn't get to vote." The others hadn't had enough time to get out of the parking lot. Jamie started for the door.

Halfway down the hallway, Zack reached for her arm but hesitated, especially after their argument last night, but the stakes were too high for her to ruin the plan he and his siblings came up with. He grabbed her wrist. "If you don't know where she is, you won't be able to give away her location and put her in danger."

"I wouldn't do that anyway." She pulled against his hold.

"If Linden and Timmins get you, they could torture you."

There were only precious seconds left to stop them. Again, she tugged her arm. "But I wouldn't—"

He cut her off. "You can't know for sure how you'd react to torture. No one does."

"Let me go!" Once she yanked free of his hold, she rushed to the door. Seconds, seconds. When she pushed, the weight of the metal door pressed her backward. A blue Expedition yielded at the end of the lot. "Wait!" she called out, but Zack's arm curved around her waist and held her in place.

"Jamie, please."

The vehicle made a left turn and disappeared with the only person she loved inside. The only person who still loved Jamie unconditionally. Tears gathered in her eyes and began falling. As she whirled around, she clenched her fists. "How could you?" She reached for his shoulders and pushed him. Of course, he barely moved. "Why? We've worked *together* all this time and now you've taken away any control I had." Again, she shoved him, this time in the chest. "Don't you understand? You've cut my heart out."

Zack leaned closer and raised his arms to reach out to her. She smacked his hands away and pounded her fists on him. Her hands ached, but she didn't care. Anything was better than the hollowness fighting for space inside her. "If anything happens to her…" She'd never forgive herself. She'd failed her sister. The possibility of failing her again by losing Charlotte was too much to bear. Jamie continued to push and shove Zack. "I hate what you've done."

"I know."

She hit him once, twice more.

Zack wrapped his arms around her, held her close. She succumbed to her worry, her fears, and accepted the comfort he offered. She cried harder but quieter. Her world had turned upside down. Again.

*God, please help me. I need You more than ever. I surrender to You.*

As her tears slowed, a soft breeze washed over her skin. The pain in her heart loosened and peace began to trickle in.

"Jamie, I promise Charlotte will be safe. The only other person I'd trust with her is Kyle, but he'll be with us."

Somehow, she knew everything would be all right. God hadn't abandoned her, just like she hadn't abandoned Charlotte. Jamie had trusted Zack enough and now her niece was safe, even if Jamie didn't know where the girl was. In her heart, Jamie believed God wanted to welcome her back to Him. Which meant He forgave her for not being there for Erin.

Maybe it was time Jamie forgave herself and gave herself permission to be happy.

And maybe saving Zack's sister was God's way of helping Jamie believe in herself again. "Thank You," she mouthed to Him.

After a few minutes more, she lifted her head. "Let's pray." Grabbing Zack's hands, she bowed her head. "Heavenly Father, Your love and support were never needed so much. Please give Zack and me the strength to protect Lily and bring Drew down so he can pay for the crimes he's committed. Take away our fears and help us to trust in You. Amen."

"Amen." Zack pulled his hands free and cupped her cheek. "You don't know how happy it makes me to hear you calling on God."

"Throughout my time with you, I've learned to trust in Him again. After all, He brought me you, didn't He?" And she'd be forever grateful.

Courage gathered inside her and started to shove through the crusted wall of guilt. Jamie *was* good enough. She would do whatever was necessary to save Lily and bring Drew to justice. And, God willing, she'd be able to pursue a happy life she hadn't felt she deserved until now.

"Okay." She slapped her hands together. "Call Kyle and the detective, then we've got to get going."

"We need a plan first." He headed back into the front office.

"We'll think of something on the way. We're running out of time."

After he glanced at the wall clock, Zack grabbed his phone from his pocket. "You lock the front door and I'll make the call."

Jamie hurried to complete her task. Behind her, Zack began a conversation with his older brother, filling him in on all that had happened since they first spoke this morning. When she turned back to the room, Zack grabbed his keys from the counter, then disappeared into the office. Thumps filtered out of the room, then she met him in the hallway. In his hand, he held a gun.

Her stomach clenched. Although she knew he wouldn't use it unless he had to, she still hated that they needed it at all. He glanced at her, then headed down the hallway to the rear exit.

They made it to Hampton Waterfront in twenty minutes. Zack pulled off the main road and drove through the loading zones. No eighteen-wheeler interfered with their travel today. Outside the windshield, seagulls drifted through the sky over the water like any ordinary day.

But it wasn't a normal day. Life was about to change. No matter what happened, she could not go back to being a fugitive on the run with her bounty hunter. And her time with the man she'd fallen in love with might be coming to an end.

Wait. She…loved him.

Her heart squeezed even more. Throughout the days, she'd felt them getting closer, had welcomed the connection. She'd grown to care for him and every moment she spent with him made her wish for many more. Yes, she loved Zack, and she'd do anything she could for him.

Zack slid the car into one of the parking spaces. Before he even shut the engine off, Jamie opened her door.

"Hey." He gripped her arm.

"I'm due in there."

"*We* are expected." He shoved his keys into his pocket.

Jamie nodded. "Right. So, let me go."

"I've been thinking. I want you to stay in the car and let me do this."

She shook her head. "They're not just going to turn Lily over to you. They want me for the exchange."

"I know. I'm still working on that part."

"Don't worry. I've got your back. I'll do whatever I have to in order to save your sister." She hadn't been able to save her own sister, but she could protect Zack's family. "I won't let you or her down." She pressed a kiss to his cheek, then rushed out of the vehicle and closed the door.

Zack stared after her. "Wait." What was she doing? The revelation hit him like a ton of bricks. She intended to sacrifice herself for his sister. "Oh, no, she's not." He couldn't lose her now. He needed her, wanted her in his life and had to have the chance to tell her so.

He grabbed the handgun from the console and hurried

out of the vehicle. Once he closed the door, he slid the weapon into the back waistband of his cargo shorts. His nerves hummed a bit more with each step closer to Jamie.

So many times, Jamie had kicked in the wall around his heart. With her passion for life, justice, her niece and through the rare glimpses of her just as a beautiful woman, she'd reminded him of the benefits of…feeling. For the past few years, he'd thought he'd be better off not getting romantically involved with another woman. But he'd changed since he allowed his work to interfere with his support of his sick girlfriend. He was responsible, trained and more mature. Yes, it was a risk and a lot could go wrong, but his need for Jamie made him want to take the chance.

"Hey." He caught up to her a few feet from the building's entrance, wrapped his arm around her waist and turned her to face him. He kissed her, deep, demanding and as thoroughly as he could. His lips pressed to hers, as though sealing the two of them together. Partners, there for each other, bringing out the best in each other. Her lips tasted sweet and loving and perfect. She gripped his shirt and kept him close. Through the kiss, he poured all his emotions into her, as though trusting her to cherish all of him as he hoped to get the chance to do with her. Fear, nervousness, hope, caring, need, faith—everything rocked inside him, but it was okay. He had Jamie by his side.

When he released her, her hazel eyes looked bewildered. Her tongue rubbed along her bottom lip.

"When we get out of this, you and I are going to have a long talk," he said.

She nodded but said nothing.

Just as well. They had to move.

For his sister and Jamie, Zack needed to focus on the rescue. The women expected him to be smart. Put his emotions in a box. Focus on the job. Professional. Cold. Nothing else.

Together, he and Jamie entered the building. Two of the lights closer to the back of the room flickered. A musty odor hit him as soon as they walked in. Squeaking noises echoed through the room. Mice, most likely.

Zack led Jamie farther into the room, then stopped a few feet behind a set of four crates with tiny labels. They only reached his waist. Where were the huge boxes they'd used for cover a few days ago?

Fear reared its ugly head as he imagined all the things that could go wrong.

Put. It. In. The. Box.

The sound of slow, deliberate footsteps floated across the floor. Linden stopped beside another set of crates a few yards away, his weapon by his side. Charlie stepped out from behind another wall of crates and dragged Lily by the arm along with him.

Immediately, Zack's heart loosened. No, his sister wasn't out of danger yet, but she was alive. Maybe he *could* get them all out safely. "You all right?"

Lil gave him a weak grin. "Of course. After putting up with you boys my whole life, this was nothing." Her words were meant to be strong, but the disheveled clothes and weary face weakened her message. No visible injuries, though. Praise God.

"I'm glad you made the right decision, Jamie," the deputy's voice boomed as he brandished his weapon.

"I'm not going to let an innocent woman suffer any longer if I can help it." Jamie stood alert, glancing around the room as though gathering intel like a seasoned soldier. Pride filled him. What an amazing woman he'd chosen to…love. He may have tried to ignore it, but he'd grown to love her and everything about her. And he wanted a chance to see what life could be like for the two of them together.

"What about the kid?"

"She's not here," Jamie stated. "You'll have to settle for me."

Zack curled his fingers. Where in the world were Kyle and Logan? The traffic jam had to be over by now. And what about Timmins? He'd been the one to call Zack about this meeting.

"That wasn't the deal." Linden turned to the other man. "Charlie?"

Charlie aimed his weapon at Lily's head.

Lil closed her eyes. With her lips moving, she was probably praying.

Zack raised his weapon. "Don't do it!" He'd been a good shot since he was nine, when Kyle and Parker first took him hunting. Both of them had called him a natural.

Never had his sister been in the line of fire, though. Would he be able to shoot straight with Lily so close?

Charlie pulled Lil in front of him, eliminating most of Zack's shot.

"Shoot him, Z!" Lily cried.

"Yeah, go ahead." Charlie snickered. "See what happens."

But he couldn't. Not yet.

Linden aimed at Zack. "There's no way out. If you shoot at either of us, I'll shoot you."

"Then I'll never tell you where Charlotte is," Zack said.

With each passing second, tension rose higher. Soon someone would fire.

*It's going to be me.*

Zack shifted his position. Shoved Jamie toward cover. Aimed for Charlie. Squeezed the trigger. Charlie dropped. His gun clacked on the floor and his mouth spouted off a load of swear words. Zack had shot him in the shoulder. One down. One to go.

Linden shot at Zack. The bullet slammed into the metal wall behind him. Then he aimed for Lily.

He had to give his sister time to reach cover. As Zack shot a barrage of bullets in Linden's direction, the deputy ducked. Lily scrambled away from the deputies. She crawled in front of the crate Linden used for cover and curled into a ball.

"Turn yourself in, Linden. It'll go easier." Zack scanned the building again. "And get your boss out here." Each moment without Timmins tightened Zack's gut.

"It's over, George." Jamie peeked around the other end of their crate. "The police are on the way."

"We are law enforcement. I'm a deputy, remember?"

Charlie struggled to move near Linden. Blood flooded the skin of his arm and the short-sleeved shirt he wore.

"No, you're just a thug following orders, committing crimes and thinking you're invincible." While he spoke, Zack pressed his back to the crate. "With the evidence we have, you guys won't be representing the law much longer." He glanced at his watch. They were sitting ducks if they didn't move. Zack stood, aimed for the deputy's hiding space. "Think long and hard about what you do next, Linden."

The lawman's arms sailed over his head, his handgun still wrapped in his fingers. "Don't shoot." Slowly he stood.

"Smart decision." Zack moved a few paces forward. He kept his finger on the trigger just in case Linden tried something. "Now, where's Timmins?" Was the man too afraid participating in the exchange would risk his "model sheriff" status?

The deputy grinned. With his free hand, Linden pointed in Jamie's direction. "Right there."

A whimper escaped Jamie's lips. Zack whirled around so he could see both lawmen.

"Take them out." With his arm tight across Jamie's shoulders, the crooked sheriff pressed a knife to her throat. "I've got what I came for."

Dread rocked inside his gut. His sister huddled by a box to his right. The woman he'd grown to love to his left. Both in danger of dying. If he shot at Timmins, he risked Jamie getting caught or stabbed and Linden shooting Lily. If he shot at Linden first, Timmins would escape with Jamie. Zack stood still, paralyzed.

"Can we hold on to the sister for a little longer?" Linden smiled. "I kind of like her."

"I don't care what you do. Just make sure she dies when you're done with her." Timmins moved the knife up and down. Jamie remained silent, but her eyes sent a message of love to Zack.

"No!"

Lily's holler grabbed Zack's attention. Charlie reached for his ankle. Linden raised his weapon. Zack scrambled out of the guys' line of fire. The deputy fired.

Zack crouched low behind the boxes. A loud bang rattled one wall. He scanned the room. Jamie and Timmins were nowhere to be seen. Another shot rang out.

His blood pumped heavier, his heart rate soaring. "Lily?" *Please, God, let my sister be all right.*

"I'm coming to you."

Zack popped up and laid down cover until Lil slid behind him. Charlie leaned to the side of his crate and shot. Bullets grazed the wood of the box they used for cover. Zack inched backward, twisted his body and covered his sister.

"It's over, Owen. You and your sister have no way out. And your girlfriend is probably already in the bay. If you surrender, I promise I'll make your deaths quick."

"There will be no deaths today," he hollered. "Not if I can help it," he added under his breath. But Jamie and Timmins had rushed out to the parking lot.

His duty was to bring criminals in to face their consequences and to protect the innocent whenever possible. *God, please guide me so I can protect Lil and save Jamie.* They were counting on him and he needed to be there for both of them.

Feet scuffled over the floor. Zack popped up. Squeezed the trigger. Hit Linden. The man's body jerked backward as his howl surged through the building. While blood stained his shirtsleeve, Linden shot toward Zack again.

The opposite door crashed open. Zack covered Lily.

"Police, stop!"

Lily and Zack glanced at each other.

"Zack? Lil?" Kyle's voice echoed off the walls.

"Over here!" Zack stood. Energy set his nerves on fire. "Lil's here. Timmins took Jamie."

"Go, go!" Lily pushed him toward the door.

Technically he could stay with his sister and let the police handle Timmins. Zack might've done that...a week ago. But a feisty, stubborn, adorable woman had crashed right into his heart. And a little girl somewhere else in the state was also counting on him to keep his promise to get them back together as soon as possible. He wanted to be the man Jamie and Charlotte could depend on.

Zack ran out the door.

Tears stung the corners of Jamie's eyes. The adrenaline began to take its toll. Her limbs felt like cooked spaghetti. She was so tired of being scared, for her niece, for herself, for Zack. She reached out to a nearby car to steady herself. If she could slow her and Drew's pace, Zack might have enough time to come for her.

"Keep moving." Drew guided her toward the bay. He'd lowered his knife but no doubt he still held it close. His hold on the back of her neck remained tight. But the pain, she knew, was nothing like what she'd experience if she couldn't come up with a way out of this.

"You won't get away with this." At least she hoped not. Jamie's stomach roiled. *Don't throw up.* "Even if you kill me, Zack and the others will make sure you pay." A pair of seagulls squawked overhead.

"Are you kidding?" he snickered. "I'm the sheriff. I can get away with anything I want."

A short wave of panic whooshed through her body. The knife Drew held returned to her neck, poked slightly into her skin.

She forced a slow breath and listened to the rhythm of the waves. Too many positives reigned over her life now. God couldn't take all that away. He wouldn't.

Faith.

"Wait. Are you praying?" Drew sneered.

*I know You're with me.*

Something shifted behind them.

"God's not on your side, Jamie."

"But I am." Zack's hardened voice drifted over Drew's shoulders. The sharp tone had never sounded so sweet.

Jamie closed her eyes and smiled. Her Zack, so calm, confident.

Drew whirled around. The hand with the knife remained by her neck. The other pinned her shoulders to his chest. "How did you…?"

"The police are here. Your deputies are already wearing cuffs." Zack took two steps toward them, a handgun wrapped in his fingers. "And we've got evidence to prove you're not the lawman you're supposed to be."

Drew continued to move away. His hand had the tiniest shiver, just enough for the blade to scrape along her neck. "Turn around, walk away and I'll consider not killing her."

"You know I can't." Zack took another step forward. "I won't let you hurt her anymore."

"You don't get it. I'm in charge here." Drew's breath slipped through her hair. He inched farther back. "Put your weapon on the ground or I'll cut a hole in her neck."

Jamie held her breath.

"Do it!" Drew scraped the blade across part of her neck, not too deep but enough to draw blood. She couldn't stop the sobs coming from her mouth.

Zack set his gun on the ground, then took another couple of confident steps toward them. "Your life's over, Timmins. Drugs, your wife, Beth McKutchen's body. We've got enough evidence to put you away for a long time."

Drew's hold on her faltered. The urge to move surged through her. Should she make an effort, shove her elbow into him? Or did Zack have his own plan?

"Trust." Zack opened and closed his fists.

"I do." She nodded. "You and God."

The building's door crashed open. Within seconds, Kyle stood to their left with his gun at the ready. To her right, Zack still moved toward them. Her brother-in-law's hold crushed her shoulders even more. His knife, though, shifted between the Owen brothers.

Now or never. Jamie bit down on Drew's forearm as hard as she could. He growled like a pit bull and released a string of swear words. She shoved his arms away. Adrenaline whooshed through her. She scrambled toward Zack. She needed to have his arms around her so much.

Zack passed her.

Fingers gripped around her shoe.

"No!" She kicked.

As quickly as the hold came, it disappeared. Something behind her thumped to the ground. Kyle ran forward, grabbed her arm and yanked her away from the others.

She swallowed the bile threatening to rise through her esophagus. Zack and Drew fought each other on the rubble pavement. With a solid grip on Drew's wrist, Zack slammed Drew's arm against the ground. The knife fell from his fingers, but the fight continued and they rolled closer to the bay.

Sirens screamed. Cars swerved somewhere in the parking lot.

"Do something!" she yelled to Kyle.

When she took a step forward, Zack's oldest brother shoved her toward the building. "Stay here," Kyle ordered.

Behind him, the scene slowed. Her hearing disappeared. Drew flipped Zack over.

Picked up the knife.

Raised it above Zack.

"Help him!" She pointed to the fight.

The scene in front of her whirled in different directions. Her heart thumped faster.

Kyle whipped around.

Zack grabbed Drew's wrist. Twisted. Fought.

Kyle lifted his weapon, but couldn't fire without the possibility of hitting his brother.

The knife disappeared from Jamie's vision. Both men stilled. Drew fell on top of Zack.

"Please, no." Who'd been stabbed?

"Zack?" Kyle's voice held as much panic as hers had. She followed him toward the fighters.

"I'm good." Zack shoved Drew off him.

Jamie's body threatened to collapse. She clasped her hands together. Bloodstains dotted his clothes and he moved a bit slowly, but her hero had survived.

As for her brother-in-law, blood spread across his shirt under the shoulder at an alarming rate. His eyes clenched.

Kyle kicked the knife away, crouched beside Drew, then flipped him over. "I've got him, little brother."

Zack closed the distance between himself and Jamie, planted his palms on her cheeks and pressed his mouth to hers. The kiss was desperate, filled with a need to connect. Her heart expanded, welcoming the emotion he poured into her. She dropped her hands on his arms. He leaned his forehead against hers. "I thought I was going to lose you."

"Never." And he wouldn't, if she had any say in the matter. In less than a week, he'd become so important in her world. "I can't imagine facing the future without you—your strength, your counsel, your lo—" Uh-oh. She raked her teeth over her lip. Heat crept into her cheeks. Zack might not be ready to hear the four-letter *l* word.

"You can say it." He smiled. "Because I love you, Jamie." He wrapped his arms around her waist, picked her up and spun her around.

As she laughed, she tightened her hold on his shoulders. "All right. I am deliriously in love with you, Zack Owen."

He set her down and kissed her again. Oh, she'd never get tired of his affections. She softly set her palm on the side of his face, under a bruise forming near his eye. He had a ripped shirt spotted with drops of blood, a slice through his forearm, too. "You're hurt."

"Not a big deal. I have you by my side and you're safe. That's all that matters." He kissed her temple. Zack's gentle words brought tears to her eyes. Her body still shook. *Don't cry. Stay strong.*

He tugged her into his arms, pulling her against his chest. She rested her head on his shoulder. The pounding of his heart slowed, almost as though her presence calmed him. Someone close by cleared a throat. Too soon, Zack released her.

"Come on. There's someone I want you to meet." He wrapped his arm around her waist and escorted her toward the building. A variety of lights flashed from around the parking lot. A man stood behind one of the cop cars. "Jamie Carter, this is Detective Logan Phillips."

Jamie assessed the man as she shook his hand. Handsome with a standard police haircut. He stood taller than everyone else, almost as tall as Parker, and with not an ounce of fat on him. "Ms. Carter, you've got a very interesting story. I look forward to hearing your side."

"I look forward to people actually listening to me."

With a sneaky sparkle to his eyes, Zack frowned. "What have I been doing since the moment I broke you out of jail?"

"Everything you could for me." She slid her arm around his waist and leaned on him again.

Detective Phillips smiled before he walked toward the officers waiting for him.

While the paramedics talked to his sister, Kyle marched right up to Zack and pulled his brother into a hug. "You've got to stop putting yourself in harm's way, you hear me?"

Jamie's eyes filled. What a strong bond the Owen family members had. Despite Kyle being leery of her, despite his refusal to assist them when Zack first brought her to the office, Kyle had come through. Maybe he wasn't as tough as he wanted the world to believe.

Once the brothers separated, Kyle stared at her. Jamie scratched her temple. After a few more seconds, he awkwardly hugged her. *Um, okay.* She accepted his kindness and patted him on the back.

"I'm glad you're all right, too. Thanks for taking care of my little brother." Without another word, he went back to Lily, who was arguing with the paramedics. She was fine, she insisted. Kyle wrapped a hand around her shoulders, spoke quietly to her and steered her into one of the ambulances.

"Wow. You've just received the Kyle Owen stamp of approval." Zack tucked her hair behind her ear.

"Should I be flattered?"

"Absolutely." He crossed his arms and kept his gaze on the gurney transporting Timmins toward the ambulance. The sheriff barked out swears and orders, but no one appeared to be listening. "Don't get too attached to Kyle, though, okay?" Zack cracked a smile.

"Don't worry. My heart belongs to someone else."

A soft breeze swept across her face. God's touch? Perhaps. She'd like to think so.

In the distance, another siren sprang to life. She pressed her palms against Zack's chest. "It's finally over, isn't it?"

He brushed his thumb across her cheek. "Yes. You'll have to face the courts for taking Charlotte, but we can probably work out a deal for you."

"Thank you."

"Thank you for being brave enough to fight for justice. And for trusting me." He kissed her forehead. "I'm sorry about the way this went down. I had hoped we'd all come out of this unharmed." He brushed his fingers over the knife scrapes on her neck.

"What are you talking about? Your sister and I are both here, safe because of you."

"Yeah but Lily's bruised and you could've been stabbed or tossed in the bay."

"Zack." She set her hands over his heart. "You made the best decisions you could with what you knew. And since Lily and I are both alive and you have my niece protected, I say you made great decisions." With another smile, she added, "Especially deciding to work with me in the first place."

Zack scanned all the activity in the parking lot, then

returned his gaze to her. "So what are you saying? You think we make a pretty good team?"

"The best."

# EPILOGUE

*Two Years Later*

From under the umbrella, Jamie glanced out over the water. The rhythm of the waves crashing onto the shore eased her heart from the hustle and bustle of day-to-day life. What a difference two years had made. She started out as a fugitive and ended up with a family. She glanced down at the ring on her left hand. Mrs. Zachary Owen. How could it already be eight months since their wedding?

She glanced up at the puffy, white clouds of a perfect summer day. God had answered her desperate pleas, just not in the way she'd expected or on the timetable she'd wanted. In the end, He'd given her the patience to wait for His perfect plan to unfold.

She and Zack dated while Drew and George faced charges, earned guilty verdicts and were sentenced to life in prison without the possibility of parole. Zack had proposed shortly after Jamie left teaching to work at a new Christian youth club. And the wedding, with Teddy Copeland and his family in attendance and Beth's mom playing the role of mother of the bride at Jamie's request, had been breathtaking at the beginning of the Christmas season. "Thank You, Father," she said simply.

Charlotte's giggle as she braved the waves on a boo-gie board caught Jamie's attention. Zack held the bun-gee cord and tugged the board over the waves. Charlotte gripped the board and laughed harder. Truth be told, Zack had been a better parental figure in the time he'd been in their lives than Drew had been for the first six years of her niece's life. Jamie sighed. Butterflies spread through her belly. Or was it movement from her son?

"You okay, there?" Lily plopped into the foldaway chair next to her.

Jamie smiled. "Yes, birthday girl."

"Don't remind me. Parker's handling it fine, but me? My last year before thirty? Yikes." Lily rolled her eyes and took another drink from her water bottle. "Where is everybody?"

Jamie buried her toes in the sand. The baby shifted again. "Kyle and Parker are playing volleyball with some friends and Jessa's taking a walk down to the breachway."

"They all left you here alone?"

"I don't mind. It gives me a chance to reflect on how awesome my life is with all of you."

"Are you kidding? You complete our family." She pat-ted Jamie's stomach. "How's my next niece or nephew today?"

"Kicking up a storm." Jamie caressed her swollen belly. "I guess he or she likes the beach."

"Still don't know what you're having?"

Jamie grinned. "I do, but Zack doesn't."

"Oh, how cruel. I know he's been excited to find out for a while."

"I only found out this morning. I intend to tell him at some point today."

Lily clapped her hands together. "Then you'll tell us,

I assume." The Owen eye sparkle gleamed. Would Jamie and Zack's baby inherit the charming trait?

Another shriek of laughter from her niece grabbed Jamie's and Lily's attention. Charlotte ran up the beach toward their blankets and umbrella with Zack on her tail. "Auntie Jamie, help!"

"Your aunt can't stop me." When they reached the umbrella, he grabbed her and tickled her sides. "I always win, sweet pea."

"I know 'cause you're a grown-up." The words floated out unevenly as a new round of laughter bellied through Charlotte.

"Not always, he's not," Kyle said from behind them.

"Charlotte, Uncle Kyle and I saw the ice-cream truck coming up the road. Want to be first in line?" Parker asked.

"Yay!" The little girl, who wasn't so little anymore, jumped and clapped.

"Guess that means yes," Parker said.

"Yeah, we should all go." Before she left her chair, Lily winked at Jamie. "Kyle's buying."

"You go and grab me something." He moved forward toward his own beach chair.

"No." Lily grabbed his wallet from one of their beach bags and then his wrist. "*We* are going to get ice cream and we'll bring something back for Zack and Jamie."

"Come on!" Charlotte grabbed both Kyle and Parker's hands. "I don't want to miss him. We could bring something back for Auntie Jessa, too." Technically Jessa wasn't an auntie, but she spent so much time with the Owen clan that Charlotte considered her family.

Parker glanced in the direction Jessa had walked, a hint of indecision whispering across his face. In a flash, he smiled and turned his attention back to Jamie's niece. "But if she takes too long, then I'll have her ice cream, too."

Charlotte pulled her uncles toward the street. "I think she'd want me to have hers, Uncle Parker." Lily and the guys laughed.

Zack dropped beside Jamie and rubbed her belly. "How's our little one doing?"

"He's moving a lot today." As she brushed her hair away from her temple, she smiled. "We should probably think about signing him up for some sports when he gets to school."

Zack stilled. "He?"

She nodded. "We're having a boy."

His beautiful green eyes widened. "Are you sure? When did you find out?"

"This morning while you were delivering a fugitive with Parker and Jessa."

"Why didn't you tell me you had a doctor's appointment? I would've come with you." He brushed his knuckles along her jawline.

"Because I wanted it to be a surprise." She slid her hand in his.

With a grin the size of the state, he looked out over the ocean. "A son."

"I'm a little overwhelmed. I know it'll be completely different than raising Charlotte."

"Don't be worried. You're great with Charlotte and this time you'll have me by your side right from the beginning." He planted a kiss on her cheek. "And the next time."

"Next time?"

"Yes." He kissed her other cheek and urged her down to the blanket. "And the time after that."

Drops of the ocean dripped from his body onto her. The touch of his cool skin sent shivers through her. "You're planning a big family, huh?"

"Big family, small family. Doesn't matter as long as I'm with you." When he stretched out beside her, he rested his hand on her expanded waist. He kissed her mouth then, a true kiss of joy, love and hope.

\* \* \* \* \*

*If you liked this book, try these other bounty hunter stories from Love Inspired Suspense:*

*HER LAST CHANCE by Terri Reed*
*BOUNTY HUNTER GUARDIAN by Diane Burke*
*FUGITIVE TRACKDOWN by Sandra Robbins*
*BOUNTY HUNTER by Lynette Eason*

*Available now from Love Inspired Suspense!*

*Find more great reads at www.LoveInspired.com*

Dear Reader,

First of all, thank you for taking a chance on Zack, Jamie and me. I'm thrilled to have the chance to share their story with you.

In *Fugitive Pursuit*, Zack's faith never wavers. When in doubt, he prays and asks for God's guidance. I wish I could be that strong every day. However, in my life I've often been more like Jamie. I, too, lost my way after a death in the family. I grew angry with God for not taking away my pain and I eventually abandoned my church. Writing this book became my path back to God. In helping Jamie heal, I learned that even in the most challenging times, God still walks with us.

I'd love to hear your thoughts about Zack and Jamie's journey. Feel free to contact me through my website or follow me on Twitter at @writercsinclair. Okay, I'm heading back into my writing cave to work on my next book.

Take care,
*Christa Sinclair*

# COMING NEXT MONTH FROM
## Love Inspired® Suspense

Available June 5, 2018

## TOP SECRET TARGET
*Military K-9 Unit* • by Dana Mentink
Lieutenant Ethan Webb is ordered to protect his ex-wife from a serial killer, but when he and his K-9 partner arrive, he discovers that private investigator Kendra Bell is posing as the target. Ethan will have to draw out a killer without losing his heart.

## VANISHED IN THE NIGHT
*Wrangler's Corner* • by Lynette Eason
After saving her from an attempted kidnapping and delivering her baby on the side of the road, Dr. Joshua Crawford feels responsible for Kaylee Martin and her newborn son. With danger dogging their every step, will he be able to protect this new family he has come to love?

## HIDDEN AWAY
by Sharon Dunn
When Isabel Connor stumbles on a smuggling ring, her only choices are to run...or die. It's a struggle for her to trust anyone, yet undercover investigator Jason Enger is the only ally she has as she flees from danger—and finds herself heading straight into a deadly storm.

## FATAL RECALL
by Carol J. Post
Paige Tatem is an amnesiac with a target on her back—and her survival depends on police officer Tanner Brody. Tanner doesn't know what she's forgotten, but he knows people will kill to ensure she never remembers—and it's up to him to stop them.

## DANGEROUS OBSESSION
*The Security Specialists* • by Jessica R. Patch
Wilder Flynn, owner of a private security company, vows to protect Cosette LaCroix, his behavioral expert, from a stalker. But can he accomplish the mission without breaking his strict code against dating employees? Or revealing the deep, dark secrets he's held close all these years?

## KILLER COUNTRY REUNION
by Jenna Night
After gunmen attack Caroline Marsh, she's stunned to still be alive—and bowled over that her rescuer is her ex-fiancé, Zane Coleman. The killers on her trail won't give up easily, and though Zane already left her once, for her own protection, he's not about to lose her again.

**LOOK FOR THESE AND OTHER LOVE INSPIRED BOOKS WHEREVER BOOKS ARE SOLD, INCLUDING MOST BOOKSTORES, SUPERMARKETS, DISCOUNT STORES AND DRUGSTORES.**

LISCNM0518

# Get 4 FREE REWARDS!

## We'll send you 2 FREE Books plus 2 FREE Mystery Gifts.

**Love Inspired® Suspense** books feature Christian characters facing challenges to their faith... and lives.

**FREE** Value Over **$20**

---

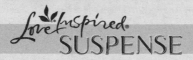
*Ethan Webb is assigned as bodyguard to a woman
impersonating his ex. Can they draw the killer out
without losing their hearts?*

*Read on for a sneak preview of*
*TOP SECRET TARGET by* Dana Mentink,
*the next book in the* **MILITARY K-9 UNIT** *miniseries,
available June 2018 from Love Inspired Suspense!*

First Lieutenant Ethan Webb brushed past the startled aide
standing in Colonel Masters's outer office.

"The colonel is—"

"Waiting for me," Ethan snapped. "I know." Lt. Col.
Terence Masters, Ethan's former father-in-law, was always
a step ahead of him. He led Titus, his German shorthaired
pointer, into the office, found Masters seated in his leather
chair.

"You're late," Masters said. "And I don't want your
dog in here."

"With respect, sir, the dog goes where I go, and I don't
appreciate you pressuring my commanding officer to get
me to do this harebrained job during my leave. I said I
would consider it, didn't I?"

"A little extra insurance to help you make up your mind,
Webb."

"It's a bad idea. Leave me alone to do my investigation with the team at Canyon, and we'll catch Sullivan." They were working around the clock to put away the serial killer who was targeting his air force brothers and sisters as well as a few select others, including Ethan's ex-wife, Jillian.

"Your team," Masters said, "hasn't gotten the job done, and this lunatic has threatened my daughter. You're going to work for me privately, protect Jillian from Sullivan, draw him out and catch him, as we've discussed."

"So you think I'm going to pretend to be married to Jillian again and that's going to put us in the perfect position to catch Sullivan?" He shoved a hand through his crew-cut hair, striving for control. "This is lunacy. I can't believe you're willing to use your daughter as bait."

"I'm not," he said. "I've decided it's too risky for Jillian, and that's why I hired this girl. This is Kendra Bell."

The civilian woman stepped into the office and Ethan could only stare at her.

"You're…" He shook himself slightly and tried again. "I mean… You look like…"

"Your ex-wife," she finished. "I know. That's the point."

*Don't miss*
*TOP SECRET TARGET by Dana Mentink,*
*available June 2018 wherever*
*Love Inspired® Suspense books and ebooks are sold.*

www.LoveInspired.com

LISEXP0518